What is it?

The earthquake had cut a jagged wound that ran across the dam from side to side. The last of the water had drained away. Heat from the dying dam rose towards Evan and seemed to push at him, and he swayed and covered his eyes. In a split second he'd seen, in the center of the dam, in the deep wet muddy part, a human form, sitting semi-upright. But its pose was deceptive. In the instant that Evan had allowed himself to look, he'd seen that it was a dead body. . . .

point

HOSTILITIES

*Caroline
Macdonald*

SCHOLASTIC INC.
New York Toronto London Auckland Sydney

"I Saw My Name in a Book" also appears in *Into the Future*, edited by Toss Gascoigne, Jo Goodman and Margot Tyrrell for the Children's Book Council of Australia and published by Penguin Books Australia Ltd in 1991. An earlier version of "The Message in the Dust" appeared in *Earthgames: A Writer's Collection*, published by Rigby Education in its Story Chest series in 1988.

ISBN 0-590-46064-1

12 11 10 9 8 7 6 5 4 3 2 1   5   7 8 9/9 0 12/0

Printed in the U.S.A.   01

For my brother, Graeme

CONTENTS

HOSTILITIES

❖

THE THIEF IN THE ROCKS

She wasn't looking forward to this trip.

Her mother said, "No, Sharon, there's no point in taking your skateboard. There'll be nowhere you can use it."

Sharon put her skateboard in the back of the station wagon anyway, propped against the picnic box. "We were going to go skating at the Dragon Room speedway today," she said as they set off. She was in the back seat.

"But you do that every day," said her father from the front seat. "This is something new."

The wide freeway seemed to stretch forever across the flat, empty country.

"Besides," her mother said, reaching back to pat Sharon's knee, "tomorrow you can go skateboarding. The Dragon Room speedway will still be there tomorrow, I promise you, and so will all your friends."

But there's all of today to get through, Sharon was thinking as the car turned off the freeway and drove past farmland.

"That's where we're going," said her father. "The You Yangs National Park."

The You Yangs looked like a pile of rubble on the skyline. As the car sped closer, the great rocks of the mountains stood out against the dark bush. The car turned into the park. "Closed at 9:30 p.m." the sign said.

Suddenly the You Yangs were towering above them. Sharon fixed her eyes on the safe, ordinary telephone box past the entrance. She felt, for a moment, frightened. She wished more than ever for the familiar danger of the Dragon Room speedway.

The car wound among the looming rocks, climbing higher into the You Yangs. They drove off the road to a picnic area. Sharon could see the plains stretching below them, and beyond the plains, the distant sheen of the sea in Port Phillip Bay. She preferred to gaze at the flat horizon than to look up at the monstrous clumps of rocks and blackened stumps behind her, but her mother was out of the car, staring upwards. "I want to climb right to the top," she said.

"You would," Sharon's father muttered. "Health freak." He got the picnic box out of the back of the station wagon. "It'll take you a couple of hours to get up there and back, so let's have lunch first."

Sharon had a sandwich and a banana, and poured herself a mug of orange juice. She wandered towards the road, considering whether it would make a suitable skateboard track. It was smooth enough, but too dangerous. Even as she stood there, a car swept around the bend and past the picnic area. She walked further along the roadway, keeping her eyes away from the mass towering above her. Then she found a perfect place. It was a wide circle of paving, forming a car park for people who were going on one of the walking tracks signposted at the edge. There was a board with a map of the area. Over on one side were parked four cars.

She ran back to her parents' picnic table. They weren't talking to each other, but at least they weren't arguing. Her father lay flat on his back along the bench, his hat over his face. Her mother was pouring herself a drink from the thermos. It was clear they wouldn't be moving for some time yet. "I've found a wonderful place to skateboard," Sharon announced, getting her board from the back of the wagon. "It's a car park around the corner."

"Are you sure it's safe enough?" Her mother craned to see where Sharon was heading, but the car park was hidden from her.

"Of course. It's nearly empty," Sharon called back.

She skated into the centre at first, then back and forth in long sweeps to each edge, looking for lumps and cracks in the surface to avoid. The paving sloped towards the board with the map, then built up steeply behind it. She developed a routine — across the car park towards the map, gathering speed, a sharp flip behind the map, then back to the cars parked on the other side.

At first she saw no other people. The whir of her wheels drowned out the hum of insects and an aeroplane heading for the airfield near by. Then she saw someone, a girl about her own age, standing alone near the edge of the car park. She wore jeans and a T-shirt, just like Sharon's, except the girl's T-shirt had painted on it a pair of red lips curved into a warm smile. The girl was smiling, too, but differently. Sharon could tell that she was laughing at her.

Sharon twirled into some complicated turns. She was annoyed. People thought she was a good skateboarder, one of the best in the Dragon Room group. There was no reason for that girl to laugh at her.

But when Sharon turned again, the girl had gone.

She heard the sound of a car approaching the car park. She coasted to the edge to keep out of its way, but sped towards it when she saw it was her parents'.

Her father spoke to her out of the driver's window. "We must have nodded off in the sun for a while. Do you know it's after four o'clock already?"

"There's still time to climb to the peak," Sharon's

mother said. Her father shook his head and looked bored. "Oh, come on, Gary," she went on coldly. "Otherwise there's hardly any point coming all this way. You might as well have slept the afternoon away in front of the TV as usual."

Sharon's father parked beside the other cars. Her mother got out of the car and strode up the track past a sign saying "Flinders Peak 40 mins." Her voice floated back to them. "We can get up there in twenty, bet you."

He followed her, after some door slamming and orders to Sharon to stow her skateboard in the back together with a reminder of its value and of the impossibility of his being able to put together that much money again to replace it should it be stolen. Sharon stood alone in the car park for a few minutes, reluctant to walk up among the forbidding rocks. Eventually she trailed after her parents. She kept her eyes fixed on the ground in front of her. It wasn't a difficult track to follow. There were steps built into the rocky surface where it became steep. The track curled around so that sometimes she could see back towards the plains and the Bay, at other times across to the tumbles of rocks on the surrounding hills.

Now that she was among the rocks Sharon felt less uneasy about them. They no longer seemed to tower overhead, threatening to overwhelm her. But even so it was startling to turn a corner and find a boulder three times her height poised at the edge of the pathway, or a sheer fall of rock held back only by a slender blackened tree trunk.

Occasionally they passed another family coming back down the path. At a narrow place a red-faced man leaned against a rock to let them pass. "Is it worth it?" Sharon's father asked him. He was red in the face himself by now.

"Great views," the man gasped.

Sharon's mother was waiting for them at the next bend, sitting on a wooden bench. Sharon sat beside her. A burnt gum tree twisted upwards from bright green bursts of new growth at its base. Beyond it she could see the pale golden plains. The glitter of sea had disappeared in the late afternoon light. The gold of the plains melted into haze which became the sky.

"Look, there's the car," her father said. Far below them was part of the car park. There were tiny vehicles parked at its edge. One of them was their bright red station wagon.

The air was still. There was silence except for the drone of a blowfly and sometimes the dry slither of a lizard in the grasses.

"Come on, Gary," her mother said. "We're nearly at the top." She stood and continued up the track. He sighed and followed her.

"I'll stay here for a while," Sharon called after them. Her legs ached. Her parents had been sleeping while she'd worked all afternoon on her skateboard turns.

The stillness continued. Then there was a movement behind her, a scatter of stones louder than the rustle of a lizard. Sharon turned her head sharply. It was that girl again, the one from the car park, on the track heading up to the peak. She was alone.

"Hi," said Sharon uncertainly.

The girl didn't seem to hear. Then, at the last moment before she rounded the curve that would take her up behind the rocks, she turned back towards Sharon. Again the friendly scarlet smile on the girl's T-shirt contrasted with her mocking grin. Then she was gone.

Sharon shrugged. The shadows around her were lengthening, darkening. It felt cooler. She shivered. Perhaps, after all, she'd follow her parents. Probably she'd meet them on their way down.

She took a last look at the toy car shining red below her from the car park, and turned to take the upward track.

Almost immediately she was confused. There seemed to be no clear track to follow. She knew, anyway, she had to keep going upwards — and around the next rock, she found she was back on the track.

Her mother had been right. The peak was very close. There was a large smooth rock to clamber over to a set of steps with an iron handrail. The steps led her to the top of a small pyramid. She found a brass plaque: "From this peak, Matthew

Flinders surveyed Port Phillip Bay 1802."

Sharon held the rail and looked around. She was higher than anything she could see.

But she couldn't see her parents. She listened. Silence. "Mum? Dad?" she called. Her voice was puny in the empty sky. Silence again. Somehow she must have missed them on the track. Well, it would be easy enough to follow the track down to the car park.

It should have been easy, but several times what seemed to be the downward track dwindled, and she was faced by rocks or was peering over a frightening drop to the bushes below. It took a long time to reach the wooden bench beside the black tree trunk. She paused to look down through the trees. There was the curve of the car park.

The car was gone.

Her heart thumped. They couldn't have gone without her? She remembered the toilet block at the side of the car park. They must have shifted the car to that side while they waited for her. More likely they were on their way back up the track to meet her. She'd hear their voices at any moment, calling her.

She continued downwards. The rocks were charcoal giants against the pale dusk sky, and their shadows were as black as the burnt stumps among them.

But sometimes the track curved upwards. Sharon was puzzled. The rocks seemed higher, too. They crowded more above her head and over the track. But then, it was getting darker, and she knew that things are different when night falls.

She turned a curve in the path. The side of the peak fell sharply at the track's edge. She could see the whole circle of the car park, lit now by two bulbs, one beside the map, one beside the toilet block. The car park was as small and remote as it had been from the viewpoint of the wooden bench. But from here Sharon could see that it was deserted. Her parents' car was gone.

She sat down on the track, her arms encircling her knees. Surely, surely they wouldn't have given up trying to find her? They wouldn't abandon her and drive off home?

Of course. She knew what had happened. They'd gone to get the park rangers or the police. If she waited here, they'd return soon. She could shout until they found her.

She knew it was better to wait. This track was so obviously not the one they'd followed on the way up. It could only lead her further astray.

She waited. Now it was completely dark. The sky was black and filled with stars. The moon was rising in a red mist from the Bay. There were stealthy rustling sounds behind her. Sharon didn't let herself look around. She stared down at the car park until the twin lights burned into her eyes. The noise is just from lizards, she told herself. Lizards won't harm me.

She had no idea what the time was. Nine o'clock
— eleven o'clock? The car park remained empty.
Then the lights went out. It seemed to signal the
end of any hope that she'd be rescued.

Sharon felt her fear build up. Don't panic! she
told herself. Calm down. She tried to think of other
reasons why the car had disappeared. Perhaps her
parents were lost, too, and someone had stolen the
car. She called out, "Mum! Dad!" Again her voice
was lost in the air, this time because it was frightened and trembling.

If only she'd tried earlier to get down to the car
park. Then she could have followed the road from
there, and found the telephone box she'd noticed
near the entrance when they'd arrived — it seemed
like a lifetime ago. Getting to the car park was
impossible now. Although the moon was higher and
touching everything with silver, it also threw enormous inky shadows. Sharon knew she wouldn't
venture into those blacknesses.

She stood up and walked a few steps, rubbing
her arms, which were prickly in the cold air. The
moonlight became brilliant, and the downward
path seemed clear and easy to follow. Perhaps,
Sharon thought, I might be able to get to the car
park after all —

The quality of the light changed to a strong yellow. A street light on top of an iron pole shone on
the track. Underneath the street light was a telephone box.

Sharon gasped with surprise and relief. The metal sides of the phone box shimmered strangely, but she didn't notice. She slid the door open. She could ring up —

No, she couldn't. She had no money. She frowned, trying to remember the emergency number that didn't need coins.

Then she noticed that the dial on the phone had no numbers. It was a blank circle. She picked up the receiver. It felt warm, as if it had just been used. She held it to her ear.

There was a swishing noise like the sea. A soft voice, full of laughter, said, "Number please?"

Before Sharon had time to get her brain working again and give her home number, she heard the phone ringing at the other end of the line. There was her father's voice. "Hello?"

"Dad!" Sharon shouted. "Oh, Dad, here I am!"

"Who's this?" His voice sounded confused.

"It's *me*. Sharon. I'm not lost at all. I'm not far from the car park."

"What? You want to speak to Sharon?"

"Dad! I'm here. Why don't you send someone to get me? It's *freezing* — " She stopped, because his voice had gone away from the receiver. He was calling from the kitchen phone up the stairwell. She could picture home so clearly from the echoes his voice made.

"Sharon!" She heard the distant words. "One of your weird friends is on the phone playing tricks.

Are you in bed yet? . . . OK, come and talk to her. And tell her it's far too late for phone calls."

"Daddy!" Sharon shrieked in the phone box. This time her voice rang and echoed. Then she heard the other voice, coming through the receiver: "Hi."

"Who are you?" Sharon asked, bewildered.

"Sharon, of course."

"What do you mean? *I'm* Sharon!"

There was a laugh on the other end of the phone that turned for a second into a roaring sound as if an avalanche of stones had plunged on to the telephone box. Then the mocking voice came to Sharon's ear again. *"I'm* Sharon now." Another laugh. "By the way, I like the skateboard. We're going to the Dragon Room speedway in the morning. Pity you can't be there."

There was a click, and the receiver became dead. "Come back!" Sharon shouted. "There's been some mistake — " But the receiver remained silent.

She replaced it, and turned slowly towards the glass door. The Dragon Room speedway. *I promise you*, her mother had said, *the Dragon Room speedway will still be there tomorrow, and so will all your friends* . . .

The light in the telephone box threw her reflection against the glass door. As she pushed it open, she saw that the great red curving smile was now on her T-shirt.

She drifted up the path, her feet hardly touching the ground. There was a night breeze stirring the new leaves of the burnt gum trees. She leaned against them, breathing in their scent.

The Dragon Room speedway? She couldn't now remember what the words meant. There were other words in her ears. She settled down in the dark shadow of a rock to wait.

Tomorrow there'd be new families coming to visit the You Yangs. Perhaps she'd like the look of one of them.

DANDELION CREEK

When we arrived at the camp site by Dandelion Creek we discovered we didn't have it to ourselves this time. Our parents groaned, but five minutes after we started unpacking they discovered that the other adults were also ex-New Zealanders and they all knew somebody who knew somebody, and next thing our camp was being set up facing theirs so there was a shared sort of courtyard area between us. "One cooking fire," I heard my father say happily. "Half the work."

We kids were more cautious. The other family had two boys. The older one was called Dunk; he was twelve, my age. The younger one was Davey and he was the same age as my sister Melissa. The adults assumed we'd all get on with each other, particularly Dunk and me — two boys the same age. Maybe we would, but not just yet.

Dunk made the first effort. "I'm glad there're other people here. I thought I'd be bored to death, just us and Mum and Dad in the middle of the bush."

I didn't know what to answer because we were used to holidays in the middle of the bush, just us and Mum and Dad, and none of us ever got bored.

The other family's presence there changed things. It was New Year's Eve, twilight. I heard Dunk's mother say, "It's all right for us — we can sit around the fire all night yakking. But what are the kids going to do?"

Normally of course Melissa and I and our older sister Laura would sit around the fire too — why not? But this time it was different. I stopped the little silence that was growing; I said, "We'll go to the picnic place and have a seance."

"They never work," Dunk said.

"If that's your attitude," I said, "naturally they won't work for you."

"Yeah — let's have a seance," said Melissa enthusiastically. As usual she was my ally.

I saw Laura frown. She was always against the idea of holding seances. "If it doesn't work, it'll just be boring," she said. "If it does work it'll scare your socks off and you'll have nightmares for weeks. It can be dangerous, you know. It's not just a game."

"If you're scared, don't come with us," I said. I could see this conversation was making Dunk and Davey really interested in the whole seance idea.

Laura didn't say any more. I think there was something else upsetting her as well. She was nearly fifteen. At that age she didn't want to be sent off with the kids, but she wasn't one of the adults, either. In this strangely altered holiday there wasn't any place for her.

She came with us. We set off before it was properly dark to a grassy patch at a bend in the river that we called the picnic place. Laura brought a rug and a torch and a book and she wore her Walkman. I followed with the cut-out letters and the numbers and the YES and NO, and a tall glass with a tiny crack in it. Melissa brought a box of kitchen candles, some matches and two candle-holders. Dunk and Davey carried the folding card-table.

We put the card-table flat on the grass and the four of us sat cross-legged around it. Laura spread her rug under a tree several paces from us and read her book by torchlight. Melissa lit two of the candles, and in their light our faces changed, became older, more mysterious. Davey's face was shaded completely as he leaned forward to place the letters in a circle on the table. Only the blond stubble on the top of his head showed.

"Leave a gap for the numbers," Melissa said.

"I know," said Davey.

"It's a mess," Dunk said. "Is that what you call a circle?"

Davey sat back, folded his arms. "Do it yourself."

Dunk pushed at the letters roughly so that the D disappeared under the C and the X, Y and Z almost fell off the table.

"Stupid idiot." Davey punched the corner of the table and all the squares of paper slid to one side. The candles tipped over.

I put my hands out and steadied the table. I'd seen the hostility simmering between the brothers even in the few hours I'd known them. I tried to speak commandingly.

"Look. This'll only work if we're calm and co-operative. The numbers and letters don't have to be in a perfect circle. It's OK as long as they're in the right order."

As I spoke Melissa put the candles upright again and she and I sorted the squares of paper. She seemed immediately to have caught my mood. Our calm movements affected Dunk and Davey and they sat watching silently.

The table was nearly ready. "Put the candles in the north and south corners," I said. I don't know what made me say that.

"Where's north and south?" Melissa asked.

I stretched an arm and pointed beyond her shoulder to where the sky still shone lighter than the black trees. "That's west," I whispered, "so the other direction's east."

Already I could feel a mysterious power hovering. My backbone straightened and I lifted my chin and stared at Melissa. Wordlessly she shifted the candles to opposite corners of the table from my outflung arms. I lowered my arms, then put the glass in the centre of the table, upside down.

"Now we place our left hands on the glass and let it know our unity, our trust, our faith in its power."

The breeze rattling the leaves had dropped and my words hung on the still air. I felt like a high priest controlling a world-changing rite. I wished I had a peacock feather head-dress, a long necklace of bones.

"My arm's getting tired," Davey said. He propped his other elbow on the edge of the table to support his left arm and everything tilted towards him.

"Davey!" Melissa wailed, grabbing the glass before it fell.

"Well, how long do we sit here? What's supposed to happen?" Davey sat back and folded his arms again.

"Typical," muttered Dunk.

My control of the ceremony was slipping away. There was a rustle in a tree near us, a hoarse breath.

"Possums!" Dunk breathed. "Let's hunt possums!"

I said in my lowest, most chilling voice, "Left hands on the glass."

Everyone obeyed.

"Is there anybody there?" I whispered.

After a couple of seconds Davey's hand wobbled on the glass and he sniggered.

"Shut up," Melissa said. "We have to concentrate."

"Ignore him," Dunk said.

"We can't," she said. "It won't work unless everyone's serious about it."

After another moment's silence, I tried again. "Is there anybody there?"

I saw Davey's arm quiver. I thought he was going to have an attack of giggles but his face close to the south candle was still, his eyes squeezed shut, his mouth slightly open. Then the glass started to move.

Slowly it circled around, sometimes jerking against the roughness in the old baize tabletop, then going faster. My forefinger lost contact briefly and I suspected someone was pushing the glass. But as it swiftly turned and rushed towards YES, there was an instant when none of our fingers was touching it.

"Who pushed it?" Melissa asked in a faint voice.

No one answered. Perhaps we all knew we were innocent. The seance was working. The glass was speaking to us. I glanced around at Laura in triumph but she wasn't taking any notice.

Our fingers touched the glass again. "Who are you?" I asked. Nothing happened for ages. We were held still in our circle of candlelight. At a farmhouse far away a dog barked, and closer there were echoes of laughter: the parents getting into New

Year's Eve celebrations. "Who are you?" I asked again, more urgently.

There was another sound, like a distant police siren. Suddenly it wasn't distant, it was shockingly close: not loud, but sharp and eerie. I heard Melissa gasp and I think I did too as I swung around.

"It's only your sister," Davey said in a disgusted voice. "She's singing with the Walkman."

"Laura?" I said to her hesitantly. I picked up the north candle and took its light over to her. She was curled up in her rug, the torch switched off, the earphones on the ground beside her. "She's asleep," I said. "It's not her." I picked up the earphones to see if the sound came from them. They were silent. The eerie whine grew quieter, then it was gone.

"Probably just a couple of mozzies," said Dunk, but his voice sounded uneasy.

I put the north candle back. We looked at each other cautiously, and stretched our hands to the glass again. "Are you going to tell us who you are?"

The glass moved sharply, jerking away from our hands. It fell on its side and instantly collapsed into a pile of glittering splinters.

We were all speechless. The south candle fluttered and went out.

"The glass tripped on a blob of candlewax, that's all it was," Dunk said. He pointed among the sharp fragments. "Remember? When Davey knocked the candles over before?"

"It wasn't my fault — " Davey suddenly stopped his protest. We heard the siren sound again, higher than before, eerier.

In a rush of movement Melissa scrambled to her feet, whimpering, "Laura, wake up!" She swooped on the huddled shape of our sleeping sister, shaking her shoulder. We were all on our feet by now. Dunk held up the north candle, sheltering it with his hand.

Slowly Laura uncurled. When I saw the look on her face I wanted to laugh. I thought she was joking, making a horror mask to give us a scare, teach us a lesson. But immediately I realised there was a terror in her staring eyes that wasn't acted.

Melissa half shrieked. I heard Davey's fearful moan, and the light wavered and nearly failed as Dunk lurched backwards.

"You're tricking us, Laura, aren't you!" She didn't take any notice of my frantic words. Her mad eyes were fixed beyond us. Then she bent forward with her palms flattened against her ears, as if she heard something too frightening to bear.

Then I heard it, too: a terrifying roar of sound. There was a monstrous revving of machinery, like a million chainsaws, which then died away just as quickly. Then there were shouts, and sounds of smashing glass, and panic-stricken screaming.

It came from the sheltered spot under the peppercorn trees, the place where the two caravans with their green-and-white canvas extensions were parked, with all the parents on director's chairs having a few wines to welcome in the New Year.

I don't know how long it went on. I don't know what the others were thinking. They were frozen just as I was. What I do know is that I wanted to escape, to run away as far as possible from the horror at the camp site.

Abruptly, it was over. Silence. The faraway dog barked once. And then, incredibly, there was a trace of laughter, my father's booming laugh, the laugh he gave only when he was in an exceptionally good mood. I could even hear music, the Roy Orbison CD that belonged to Dunk and Davey's parents.

Dunk dropped the candle and it died, but it didn't matter. The moon had sailed out from behind the trees or clouds or wherever it had been hiding. In its light I could see the others' shocked faces.

"What was *that*?" Dunk gasped. "It sounded like an attack on the camp!"

So they'd heard it too. I hadn't imagined it.

"It can't have really happened, though, can it?" Melissa said, her voice trembling.

"Of course not," I said. "Maybe it was something they played on the CD." What I really thought was that it had something to do with our seance.

"I want to go back now," Melissa said in a baby-girl voice I hadn't heard her use for years.

"OK," I said. I knelt by Laura. "Are you OK now,

Laura?" She seemed to be asleep again. I touched her shoulder and then drew back sharply. She was very cold. She wasn't breathing.

"Melissa. Go and get Mum. Quickly. Tell Dad to call an ambulance." I tried to keep my voice calm.

"Is she *dead*?"

"Just hurry, Melissa. Remember, tell Dad to get an ambulance."

The boys went with her. I watched them speeding along the path in the moonlight. The thudding of their feet was as rapid as my heartbeats.

I covered Laura with the sides of the rug she was lying on, hoping she'd feel the warmth. I didn't know what else to do. I could see now that she was breathing, but very faintly. She was so cold. I found the matchbox and lit one of the candles. Her face was deathly white. The seance had done this to her. It was all my fault.

There was another rush of footsteps and my mother was beside me, crouching over Laura, stroking her forehead, checking her pulse. "What's been happening here?" she asked, and it seemed to me like an accusation.

"I don't know."

She looked at me, and now her voice had its normal gentleness. "Poor Andrew. You look petrified. Don't worry. Peter's called for an ambulance on his car phone, and it won't take long for it to get here from town. I'll tell you what, why don't you go up to the road and wait for it? It'll save time if you can guide the driver down here."

She turned her attention back to Laura, and I left them there in the glow of the single candle.

I took a short cut through the bush to the gravel road that led from the main road to the camp site. I could see back to the firelight at our camp, and beyond that the shine of moonlight on the creek.

There was another light in the thicker bush on the other side of the camp road. It was a gleam like a slow-moving torch or a glint on metal, and I strained my eyes to see what it was because I thought we were the only campers in the area.

Then I saw clearly the whole glittering menace. They moved among the trees with perfect guerilla stealth, sitting on their silent motorbikes, inching forward with their feet. Some of them carried loops of heavy chain. They all wore sinister black balaclavas with three holes for eyes and mouth. They stole through the bush in an arc centred on the camp site under the peppercorn trees.

I had a dizzying feeling that time was running backwards, that the sound of battle had happened too soon. But I knew the noise we'd heard had been some kind of trick of our imaginations, maybe a trick of the spirits we'd summoned in our seance.

This wasn't a gathering of spirits. These were real bikies, bushranger bikies, and they were going to attack our camp site.

I opened my mouth and a scream of warning and fury poured out as I ran towards the light of the camp fire. The arc of invaders stopped and their faces turned to me. I saw their eyes glitter. I kept on shouting. The adults by the fire peered around, their night vision weakened by the bright flames.

I thought I'd stopped shouting to catch my breath as I ran, but the sound went on and on. Then I realised — it wasn't me, it was the siren of the ambulance. It was a long way from us, maybe still back on the main road, but its noise cut through the night air.

At the sound of the siren, the gang swung their motorbikes around. In a second the roar of ten or twelve ignitions drowned the siren, drowned even the shouted curses and insults from the riders, the scatter of gravel when they hit the camp site road. They were in retreat.

As the clamour of the motorbikes faded, the ambulance siren grew louder. My father shook me to drive away the shock and stop my shouting. "What the hell happened?"

"Bushranger bikies," I said at last, still gasping. "Closing in on our camp. Frightened off by the siren. Must have thought it was the cops."

"Frightened off by your yelling, more like it," my father said. "I've never heard such a bloody row." He was trembling nearly as much as I was. I saw him exchanging glances with the other parents. Davey and Dunk were gaping at me. "Come on, lads," their father said. "Help us get packed up." And amazingly, Davey and Dunk did help, immediately, without arguing even between themselves.

Melissa stared at me and clung to Dad, and I knew (I think) what she had in her mind — she wasn't sure if the shouts and noise she'd just heard were any more real than the previous lot.

As the ambulance approached the camp site, Mum and Laura came walking very slowly along the track, Mum with her arm around Laura's shoulders. She was still ghost-white, and very weak, but she had enough spark in her to hiss at me, "I told you it was a dangerous game."

"Yes, but it gave us a *warning*," I hissed back.

Mum was urging Laura towards a seat by the fire and I don't know if either of them heard me. Melissa did, though. She understood.

"It was a kind spirit, then, wasn't it, Andrew? It gave us a pretend scare so we'd be ready for the real one."

"Something like that," I said.

We packed up and left the camp site in a record time of eleven minutes. The ambulance crew took Laura and my mother with them. They couldn't wait to see us leave safely. New Year's Eve was their busiest time of the year, they said, but they radioed the town police about the bushranger bikies.

My father said that such a bad-luck camp site was no place to see in the New Year and it was essential we were gone before midnight. I'm glad we left. I don't think any of us would have slept easily.

THE GREENHOUSE

Late last year my uncle Jim and aunt Elaine bought a block of land. It's an orchard very like all the other blocks around it in this country area near Tauranga. There's a pleasant house near the road. Behind it are rows of orange and mandarin trees, groves of avocados; and beyond them are four greenhouses and two stretches of kiwifruit vines. The ground is neat and level. Nothing unusual about the block at all. Or so it seemed.

They invited me to stay with them at the new block during the school holidays. We called it a working holiday, but really I didn't have to work too hard, just help with whatever was being done from day to day. A crop of tomatoes was nearing its end in one of the greenhouses. They were dark red and strong-flavoured. "The perfect tomato," Jim said (we're not into titles like Uncle and Auntie in our family), polishing one with his cloth gloves. He told me that they were fetching good prices at the local market and at the roadside stall by the gate.

I helped Elaine pick tomatoes in the early morning. The outside air was around freezing point, but inside the greenhouse it was steamy. The tomato plants were dense and reached high above our heads. Their late-season leaves, some of them drying and silver-brown, rustled together as we walked in, although there was no breeze.

Elaine turned on the radio she was carrying and set it in the aisle that ran down the centre of the greenhouse. A political correspondent's voice boomed out the latest on student unrest in China. "I like the radio loud in here," Elaine shouted.

We started picking, one each side of the centre aisle. I tried not to shudder at the disgusting feeling when my fingers sank into an overripe tomato, not to flinch and squeal when trailing leaves caught in my hair as I pushed between the dense rows. Standing on rotten tomatoes was upsetting, too. They seemed to resist, then burst with a sickening splurt of juice and pips.

"It's good to have some company in here," Elaine called. She was ahead of me, working through the rows more quickly than I. "I've never managed to get to the end of the greenhouse before it's time to quit."

I couldn't even see the end of the greenhouse, either end. "When's it time to quit?" I called back, trying to keep the hope out of my voice. The build-up of heat was awful. It made my eyes go funny. Sometimes the gleaming tomatoes seemed to dance in front of me and I'd find I was trying to pick a handful of air.

"When it gets so hot it's unbearable," I heard.

That was right now, for me anyway. I headed for the sound of the radio. The plants seemed to have crowded into the centre aisle even since we'd started. I dodged the full containers of tomatoes left at the end of every second row and collected my jumper from the ground near the door.

The sharp frosty air outside was heaven. Elaine appeared beside me. "Taking a rest?" she shouted over the orchestral music. "Good idea. Your face looks very flushed. I'm just going to shift the radio."

The nose faded as she vanished into the greenness with the radio. Both she and the music were absorbed by the murmuring leaves and the sultry air. I had cooled down now, and thought I could manage to pick a few more rows.

Back in the greenhouse I couldn't find where I'd left off picking. Rows I *knew* I'd picked were again hung with red perfect tomatoes. Had I really missed so many? I decided to start again near Elaine, and kept walking towards the sound of the radio. But I noticed that Elaine had missed as many tomatoes on her side as I had on mine. It looked as if nobody had been picking there this morning. It didn't seem to matter where I started.

At last Elaine said we'd done enough for the day. As she'd predicted, we hadn't reached the end of the greenhouse. We carried the full containers out and loaded them on to the trailer for Jim to pick up with the tractor.

"Tomorrow," Elaine said as we walked back to the house, "we'll start at the other end. That is, if you can stand another morning of it." Peggy the corgi hurried from the house and rolled in the grass at our ankles. "Even Peggy hates that greenhouse, don't you Peggy?"

The next morning was the same. "I've never seen a crop like this one," Elaine shouted over "Rural Report." "It should have been finished three weeks ago."

By the time we were overwhelmed by heat, the end of the greenhouse was not even near. And so it continued for two more days. The slush underfoot of rotten fruit built up, we loaded hundreds of buckets of tomatoes on to the trailer, and yet the branches were still covered with ripe fruit. We never reached the other end.

On the fifth day I suggested that Elaine and I start at opposite ends of the greenhouse on the same side, and pick towards each other. The idea was that we'd stop when we met. Well, we never reached each other. I could hear her radio, but no matter how fast I picked, the sound was no closer. I went back to the centre aisle to go and find her. Immediately I was confused. Which end had I started from? Which side had I been picking? I couldn't get any clues from the plants. Everywhere I looked they were covered in pickable fruit.

On the sixth day Elaine went to golf. I dawdled on the way to the greenhouse on my own. There was a cold wind funnelling between the rows of orange trees. I approached the greenhouse as if it were an enemy.

Part of the tin moulding from the apex of the roof hung down sideways and moved gently as the wind caught it. For the first time I noticed how many of the glass panes were missing or broken. This greenhouse was far more dilapidated than the others. Jim had told me that they nearly hadn't bothered to plant it because there'd be too much damage from birds feeding. But I saw how the birds stayed away.

I started picking. As usual I peeled off my jumper at the end of the first row. At the end of the third row I was confused. Already I couldn't see the end I'd started from. I couldn't see where I'd left my jumper.

I realised why Elaine brought the radio and I wished I'd brought it with me today. It was a reference, a point of sound that helped you remember where you were. I started picking down the next row in the silence that was not quite silent. There was an eerie rustling of leaves, but all around me the leaves were still. Faintly I could hear the rushing of the wind outside and from time to time something else: a drawn-out squeak like the chilling sound of a door slowly opening — or closing — on rusty hinges.

The heat was pushing at me in waves. It was time to leave. I couldn't remember which way to turn to get to the centre aisle. The tomato plants crowded and now I could see their leaves rattling as if they jostled against each other in their hurry to surround me. The fruit multiplied and reddened almost in front of my eyes. The fingers of my picking gloves were stained red and dripped with the juice of the overripe fruit I pushed through to find a way out. The plants had joined above my head. The rustling of the leaves became deafening.

And then: quiet. A hush. I'd found the aisle. I could see the glass roof again above me, and through it the clouds hurrying in the strong wind. I could breathe more easily.

The quietness was broken. I heard the strange screek of the door with the rusty hinges and for an instant I panicked. But then I could see what was causing the sound. It was the tin moulding from the roof scraping across a pane of glass, pushed back and forth when a stronger gust of wind caught it. Suddenly everything seemed normal again, and I smiled. There was always a rational explanation, even if sometimes it was hidden for a while.

And so I decided this greenhouse wouldn't defeat me. I would not let its threatening crop overpower me. I was determined to stay there and pick until

I reached the other end. I decided that if I picked just those plants beside the aisle, I would reach the other end of the greenhouse before the heat got to me.

Half an hour passed. I lost count of the buckets of tomatoes I'd picked and left along the aisle. When I looked back they were lost in the crowding plants. The aisle seemed to be closing in behind me. I couldn't see the end, but it *had* to be close.

I was tired. My ambition to reach my target fought with my exhaustion. Then I noticed the smell.

It was a smell so strong that I could almost see it. It had easily enough power to cover the sweetish smell from the rotting fruit. It was the stench of a terrible, unthinkable decay, and it was somewhere close. It was menacing, growing.

I ran. The heat was blinding. Crazily I thought the tomato plants were trying to stop me. Perhaps I screamed. I heard Peggy barking, and there was the door at the end of the greenhouse standing open, and Peggy barking and growling a short distance outside. She stood angrily stiff on her short legs.

I crouched on the cool grass beside her, patting her and smoothing down the ridge of hair that stood erect along her backbone. We were both trembling.

"Are you all right?" I heard. Behind us was the woman who lived on the next-door block. She was at her clothesline, gathering armfuls of sheets that were flapping in the wind.

I nodded. I couldn't speak because I was still gasping, trying to breathe properly.

"It's that greenhouse, isn't it?" she went on. "Well, your uncle'll learn it's best to leave that one alone."

She was nodding to herself as she lifted her basket of washing and went. Peggy and I went, too. We passed the greenhouse with its broken panes and creaking iron, went through the orange trees and avocados back to the house.

Jim was there, speaking on the phone. I started squeezing some oranges for a drink and presently he found me in the kitchen. "Tomatoes," he said, in a disgusted voice.

"Yes," I said. "I've picked quite a lot, but I haven't loaded them on to the trailer."

"Forget it," Jim said. "That was the market manager on the phone. That last lot of tomatoes I took in to the market rotted before they got to the auction floor. Had to be dumped. Waste of petrol even driving them in."

Elaine arrived back from golf. "I checked the stock on the stall," she said, "and look." She held up one of the clear plastic bags of tomatoes we'd packed yesterday to sell on the roadside stall. Now the bag held only a black liquid mess, and it stank. "They're all like that," she said. "They're seeping out of the bags all over the stall. We'll have to clean it up."

"You're picking them too ripe," Jim said.

"We're only picking the firm ones," Elaine replied, narrowing her eyes at him.

"One more pick," Jim said. "One really hard pick tomorrow and make sure you get that greenhouse cleaned out. It's time that crop was knocked over." He was clearly upset by the phone call.

"Don't talk surly to me," Elaine said. "You've never picked in that greenhouse." She and I looked at each other.

"All right!" Jim waved his arms. "Tomorrow I'll drop everything else! I'll leave the million-and-one other jobs that are crying out to be done everywhere I turn around this place and come and help you!"

"Good," said Elaine.

The next morning we all set off: Elaine with her radio, Peggy, Jim and I. As usual Peggy stopped a long distance from the greenhouse. This time, after a few more steps, we all stopped.

It was that stench, a stink a thousand times more concentrated than the one from the plastic bag. It was the stench from yesterday in the greenhouse, but now it had gathered strength and it rolled out to meet us. The sun glinted on the panes and for a second it looked as though the contents of the greenhouse were burning.

Jim pinched his nose with thumb and forefinger and pushed open the door. Inside was black ruin. The plants were burnt skeletons swaying from their strings. The ground was a glittering, oozing tide of rot. It was as if a dreadful tide of frost had blasted the crop with the force of a nuclear fire.

Jim stepped back and kicked the door shut. The whole frame of the greenhouse shook and the stink increased. There was nothing to say, and we trooped back to the house.

Of course there were other things to be done around the orchard block. But over the next few days the smell seeped through the orange trees and the avocados and hung like a shroud around the house. Jim gathered together some gear and said he was off for a few days' trout fishing. Elaine arranged a week's golfing trip up north with her cousin. As for me, the school holidays were over. I was due home.

I remember planning, during the bus trip home, to return to my uncle's place next holiday and find out about the greenhouse. That neighbour obviously knew something. I could talk to her and some of the previous owners of the block. I had an idea of a kind of haunting, some terrible deed committed on that square of land in the past. Maybe murders, buried skeletons. I really wanted to uncover the mystery.

But when I got home and was sitting at my desk in our tenth-floor apartment in Auckland, looking out at the cool sunsets of early spring, I couldn't recapture the panic I felt. The strength of the heat and the stench seemed improbable. I couldn't see why I lost my way in a few rows of tomato plants.

I had tried to forget the whole thing. But I've just got a letter from Elaine, and the disturbing feelings are alive again.

Elaine tells me that the smell had quite disappeared by the time she arrived back from her golfing trip. There was only the heavenly scent of smoked trout from Jim's catch in the smoking shed outside the back door.

She writes that Jim had to come home a day early from his fishing trip because that old tomato greenhouse mysteriously burst into flames in the middle of the night. The neighbours called the fire department, but the greenhouse was a dying heap of ashes and broken glass long before the fire engine arrived.

Quite a relief, Elaine says in her letter. They had no plans to replant that old greenhouse.

But they've had a good year for kiwifruit, she continues. They've got enough money to bulldoze the land where the greenhouse used to be and put in a swimming pool, a good deep one, deep enough to dive into.

I'm not swimming in that pool, ever.

THE DAM

After the air-conditioned coolness of the bus and the softening tint of its windows, the glaring white heat of South Australia, midsummer, pushed against the boy so he seemed to sway and nearly fall as he stepped down to the roadside.

No one waited to meet him. There was nobody anywhere around. The bus rushed away and the boy felt that it took with it the last people he'd ever see.

Across the road was a café for truckies. It seemed to be abandoned but as the boy watched a man opened the café door, stood with his hand shading his eyes, and shouted across the shimmering stillness — "Are you the kid that wants a lift to old Meredith's?"

The boy tried to shout "Yes," but his throat had

closed in the dryness so he settled for an energetic nod.

"Well, come on, then. Over here into the ute."

The boy picked up his suitcase and crossed the road. The man sat in the cab of a dirty yellow ute parked in the shadow of the café. "Put your bag on the back, mate, and hop in. What's your name?"

"Evan," the boy said.

"You look a bit young to be after a job at old Meredith's."

"I'm not going for a job. It's a holiday. She's my aunt."

"Your auntie? Well well. So you're young Ellie's lad. Been here before?"

"No. Actually this is the first time I've been to Australia."

"Yeah? So where did young Ellie fetch you up then?"

"New Zealand."

"No kidding. Tell you what, say 'fish and chips' for me."

Because it was the third time Evan had been asked this since he landed in Adelaide the day before, he just laughed and pretended to be interested in the countryside they were driving through, the pale earth with even paler patches of dry grass.

"I reckon your mum would notice a few differences at old Meredith's place since she grew up. That's for sure. Things have changed since young Ellie used to come home from school for the holidays. Yep, she'd see a difference in the old property these days."

The ute stopped in a swirl of pink dust. "There y'go," the man said. "Along that track you'll find the house. I don't drive up there. The potholes'd do in me axle."

"Thank you very much for the ride," Evan said.

"No trouble. I always come this way. Besta luck."

His aunt Meredith was about sixteen years older than Evan's mother, which still shouldn't have made her all that ancient.

Well, she looked about a hundred. And her old house with its long dim verandas was forbidding in its total silence. Evan's high-laced runners squawked on the wooden floors and he couldn't find a way to walk soundlessly.

"This will be your room," she said. The room was empty except for an enormous bed standing high above the floor. "Put your things in the corner for the meantime. Maybe I'll find a cupboard or a set of shelves for you."

She frowned when he sat on the edge of the vast bed and bounced. But all she said was, "You'll need some proper boots for the farm. Not those fancy rubber things."

There was no television, he noticed, when he followed her through a dark sitting-room full of leather chairs and wooden sideboards all looking black in the gloom, nor any sign of a telephone.

The kitchen was light and filled with heat. The late afternoon sun fell in squares on the wooden floor, and across a table showing its soft pale surface from scrubbing. There was a large sink with one tap. Most of the heat came from a wood-burning stove. Aunt Meredith filled a kettle from the tap, set it on the stove. "We'll need wood," she said, pointing with her foot at the box on the floor by the stove.

The late sun's rich gold reached through the windows and touched her long black skirt and jacket, giving them a rust-coloured glow undershot by a navy-blue sheen. Her short hair, which Evan had seen as old and white, now shone golden. Her long nose and strong jaw were pale and young looking against the shadows on the rest of her face.

"Well, Evan, why are you staring so? You look as if you've seen a ghost. That way, outside the back door, you'll find more wood."

From the back veranda the ground stretched away, a grey-gold emptiness to the hazy blue on the horizon. *There'll be birds there*, his mother had said, *Australia is full of wonderful birds*, and she'd made sure he'd packed his bird-watching field-glasses, as if he'd be likely to forget them, and given him a book on Australian birdlife. She couldn't have known there'd be this emptiness, this hot silence. Or had she forgotten what it was like?

At least the house had electricity. After sunset the harsh white light on Aunt Meredith sitting opposite him at the kitchen table made Evan wonder how he'd been able to imagine that young sunlit face. When they finished eating dinner, she selected a small set of drawers from another room, and together they carried it into his bedroom.

When they were back in the kitchen, she said, "I hope you'll have an enjoyable time here. But I must say I'm still not sure why your mother sent you to me."

"She said it was time I found out about my Australian relations," Evan said. He didn't add that she'd asked him to find out if Aunt Meredith was OK, and to make sure that the farm Aunt Meredith loved too much to leave was going as well as ever.

"She said you should find out about your Australian relations, did she?" Aunt Meredith stood up and touched the table with the tips of her fingers. "Well, maybe you will, maybe you won't. My attitude is, what you can't work out for yourself, you don't deserve to know."

She seemed to expect him to go to bed when darkness fell. "Goodnight," she said, standing with her hand on the kitchen light switch, looking at him expectantly, waiting for him to go to his room.

Evan had never slept in such a huge expanse of bed with seven pillows as well. He was tired after his journey but sleep wouldn't happen. There were bay windows facing the side of the bed and for a while he lay looking out at the emptiness, its earlier grey-yellow turned silver in the starlight.

At last he fell asleep and dreamed of water, a deep pond of brown water in the middle of barrenness, nothing like the lake at home: clear depths surrounded by dark bush and teeming with birdlife. This strange brown water beckoned his dream self. He teetered on its steep bank of dry yellow.

Then his eyes were open. The silvery night outside the window had changed to the pinkness of dawn. The bedroom door was open. His aunt stood there.

"Never sleep with your feet pointing to the window," she said. "It's too dangerous."

Evan woke properly and sat up. Were those words part of his dream? The door was open and he knew he'd closed it last night, but his aunt wasn't standing there. During the night he'd wriggled around in bed, clutching one of the pillows. In the morning light he realised he lay across the bed, his feet pointing towards the window.

There were sheep to be fed with bundles of lucerne from the barn. Aunt Meredith showed him what to do but she didn't help. She released the chooks from their hut where she'd enclosed them before sunset to protect them from foxes.

After breakfast she said she'd show him around the farm. She glared at his runners but he had nothing else to wear on his feet. "We'll have to walk," she said. "I've sold all the horses."

She took him to a dam that lay in a fold of the

empty yellow land. Its baked clay sides were the same as those he'd seen in his dream, and so was the brown water, but the water was only a tenth of the dream volume.

"The dam's leaking," said Aunt Meredith. "This is my great problem."

The water looked like liquid mud. In the sunlight it had an oily blue-green sheen.

As Evan leaned forward to look, grasping at the shadows of his dream, his foot slipped and a small avalanche of yellow earth opened air under his feet. As he teetered, there was a slither of strong movement, a snake dancing almost at his toes.

Aunt Meredith grabbed his arm, stopped him from falling and drew him upwards to the edge of the dam. Evan was crushed against her. He felt the boniness of her shoulder and smelt the musty blackness of her jacket.

"A tiger snake," she said. Evan looked down at the elegant mark its slither made on the fine dry mud. "There wasn't enough water for my horse, but still the snakes keep alive. I told you that you need proper boots."

She led him back to the house. She said there wasn't much else to see. She said he could spend the rest of the day working in the shadehouse. He didn't bother to ask her about birds.

The shadehouse grew vegetables. Dry yellow cabbages and broccoli and tomato plants struggled against an onslaught of weeds. After two hours

Evan's back ached and his hands were dark green and throbbed from the stinging rasps of sticky grass. He wondered if this was what his mother had meant by an Australian holiday learning about Australian birds.

"I found you some boots," Aunt Meredith said. The boots sat in the centre of the kitchen floor. They were grey with age, and cobwebs crisscrossed the tops. "You'll need to black them. Then they'll soften up."

Evan measured the sole of one of the boots against the sole of his runner. After all, he thought, no point in cleaning them up if they aren't going to fit.

The boot looked about the right size. It was laced with a long strip of leather — kangaroo hide, Aunt Meredith told him. Evan eased both boots open and shook them upside down. He peered inside them in the light from the window. No spiders, no scorpions.

"Have you ever slaughtered a sheep?" Aunt Meredith asked as he spread strong-smelling black shoe polish liberally across the toes of the boots. "No? I'm surprised. I thought New Zealand was full of sheep. Anyway, you might have to learn how if we're going to continue to eat."

She's joking, Evan told himself. The blackness he brushed on the leather seemed to make the boots come to life with suppleness. It was important, he felt obscurely, that every crack and crevice in the leather be anointed and then gently coaxed to a brilliant shine.

He took off his runners, tried on the boots. They were an exact fit. He strode around in a circle. "Perfect," he said to Aunt Meredith.

It was late afternoon. Again in that light the aunt's hair was golden. Evan forced himself to stop staring at the transformation. He looked at the floor, then bent to start undoing the hard leather thong shoelace. "Shall I feed the sheep?"

"No. Feed them only in the morning," she said. "But you can close up the hens. Leave your boots on. There might be snakes this time of day, you know, looking for eggs."

The chooks seemed to know it was time to go to bed. He didn't have to chase them.

The waning light touched the empty fields with blueness. It gave them a beauty he hadn't seen before. Evan wished he had a dog and a horse. It would be nice to slap his thigh and say, "Come on Bluey," and ride off to check the rest of his land.

Even without a dog, Evan was drawn to the dam. The sky was pale blue with red streaks from the west; the land was dark. Evan strode over the dryness. He could smell the water in the dam.

"Evan!" he heard. "It's getting dark! Come back!" It was Aunt Meredith. He paused, turned back, aware of the pull of his feet to continue. He saw the sudden violet velvet of the sky. In a moment it would be dark. He could get lost. He went back to the electric lights of the house.

He liked his boots. He placed them on the floor by the window so he'd see them as soon as he woke. He was exhausted and fell asleep easily.

In his sleep the dam called him. It was filled with water in his dream, so full that the water lapped at his boots and its surface rippled clear blue in the breeze. Across the water stood a young woman. It was Aunt Meredith, the young Aunt Meredith he'd seen in the late afternoon sunlight. She saw him. "Why are you following me?"

The threat in her voice made him run, as fast as he could, back to his bed. He placed his feet well away from the window.

In the morning he was woken by the excited song of magpies, and drowsily he thought maybe there are birds here, after all — then the sounds changed and he could hear Aunt Meredith's voice. Again, oddly, the door was open. She wasn't speaking to him. He heard her say his mother's name — Ellie — and he sat up eagerly, thinking she was talking to his mother on the phone — then, disappointed, he sank back on the pillows as he remembered there was no phone. Aunt Meredith was talking to herself.

While they were having breakfast, Evan held his cup of tea firmly in both hands and told her that this wasn't really what he'd expected of Australia.

"From what Ellie told you, no doubt." His aunt looked severe. "Well, of course, Elspeth always had a very romantic view of all this. She went off to boarding school and came here only for vacations. And back then it was — richer. Greener. There were horses to ride, flowers in the garden."

"Birds?" said Evan.

"She told me that birds are your special interest. There were birds here then, more trees. Parrots. All colours. Galahs. Cockatoos. Crop nuisances, mainly."

"Mum's your half-sister, really, isn't she?"

Aunt Meredith didn't answer for a while. She spread her short work-roughened fingers on the table and Evan wondered if she would refuse to talk about the family.

"My mother," she started at last, "was widowed, when I was fifteen. My mother then went out and got herself a new husband. A young twerp years younger than she. Maybe she thought the property needed youth and strength. I don't see why she would have thought that. I'd been doing the work of a man around here since I was twelve."

"So he was my grandfather?" Evan prompted.

"Oh yes. He was the father of your mother." Aunt Meredith's voice was bitter.

"What happened to him?"

"He disappeared. A motoring accident, they said. Well, he used to drive like the devil. Perhaps he wandered away from the wreck and collapsed. He'd be carried off in pieces by crows and dingoes."

Evan shuddered. "Didn't they find him?"

"No," she said.

Evan could tell that she'd hated his grand-father.

"My grandmother died quite early, too, didn't she?" he said. "Mum said she never knew her. Mum said you were more like a mother to her, that you brought her up, really."

"She died," Aunt Meredith said loudly, "the day before her flashy young husband did his disap-pearing act. I told you they said it was a motoring accident. Maybe it was, or maybe he ran away. He can't have expected his new wife to die of pneu-monia so soon and leave him with a couple of orphaned girls. She left him everything in her will, and he didn't even stay long enough to pay his respects at her funeral."

She stood up, gathered the plates on the table to take to the sink. "Time to feed the sheep. And I wish you'd keep away from what's left of the dam. There's not enough water for me to be doing un-necessary washes to get mud off your clothes."

Evan had been hoping to steer the conversation to a question about going to the nearest town, to the pictures maybe, or even just to see some other human beings. But it was hard to find the right words, and anyway, it was clear she'd decided that their conversation was over.

* * *

After another boring day he almost looked forward to the confusion and adventure of his dreams. He'd kept away from the dam, as she'd asked. He'd worked in the shadehouse, ignoring the persistent pull, the urge to walk away that he was sure came from the pleasure of new boots.

His aunt could put no such prohibition on his dreams. Again he was at the edge of the dam as it used to be, full of water, sparkling. He knew there were birds about even if he couldn't see them yet, didn't want to look, because a young and fierce Meredith strode towards him and forced him to listen to her words. *You can't sell this place. You can't just sell our land and run off with the money. I won't let you.*

She held something sharp and heavy, which loomed towards him.

There was darkness, then a burning red pain in his chest and brilliant flashes behind his eyelids. He was crushed on all sides by water, lost under an ocean with no boundaries. And then, as the red pain subsided and the flashes in his brain dimmed, he didn't care any more about finding air to breathe. He was now part of the water.

Then, half asleep, aware that he was alive and safe in bed but not properly awake, he re-enacted in his mind the delicious moment when he stopped fighting and gave in to the power of the water. He told himself that this was what it would feel like to die by drowning.

Evan opened his eyes. He saw the starlight streaming in, and found that he was twisted around in the giant bed again. In fact the bed itself seemed to be several paces closer to the window. He sat up, fearful, wondering if he should push it back to its proper place in the centre of the room.

Wide awake — he was sure he was now wide awake — he felt a savage tilt and a roundabout movement as if the floor was alive and dancing. He leaped for the doorframe, spread himself under it, his back pressed to the closed door. An earthquake, in Australia? He anticipated them at home, knew how to protect himself. But here?

Some minutes passed and nothing more happened. He crept back to bed and snuggled among the pillows. Perhaps it had been part of his dream, and just as meaningless.

"While you slept," Aunt Meredith said as they had their breakfast, "there was a slight earth tremor. Maybe something to do with the drought."

The earthquake wasn't a dream, then. Evan thought about this several times as he worked through the tasks she'd set him in the shadehouse. But he wanted to look at the dam once more. He didn't realise this until he was walking towards it. By now his boots were dulled by dust but their suppleness remained and they enclosed his feet as gently as gloves.

The earthquake had cut a jagged wound that ran

across the dam from side to side. The last of the water had drained away. Heat from the dying dam rose towards Evan and seemed to push at him, and he swayed and covered his eyes. In a split second he'd seen, in the centre of the dam, in the deep wet muddy part, a human form, sitting semi-upright. But its pose was deceptive. In the instant that Evan had allowed himself to look, he'd seen that it was a dead body.

A rusting hunk of iron machinery pinned the body into the mud across its hips. There was no flesh left on the jaws and cheekbones that glared at Evan, or on the shoulders, just a covering of mud that, to Evan's eyes, seemed to take flesh's place. Shreds of some kind of jacket hung across the chest. The legs stuck straight ahead and had remains of trousers. The two feet sat upright on their heels, fragments of grey sock drifting from the toes.

Evan remembered his dream of drowning, and knew that the boots he wore were made first for those feet. He remembered Aunt Meredith's words: *What you can't work out for yourself, you don't deserve to know.*

He forced his eyes open again. The floor of the drained dam was smooth, broken only by the crack from the earthquake. There was no sign of the body now, not even a bone or the skull. Nearly forty years at the bottom of the dam had reduced his grandfather to nothing.

Memories of his disturbing dreams became

sharper, and mingled with the other things Aunt Meredith had told him. Inside his head he could see the young Aunt Meredith whom he'd met in his dreams and seen sometimes in the angles of late sunshine. *I had to kill him*, she said. *He would have taken everything.*

Evan looked around at the drought-stricken land. The farm was lost now, anyway. He wondered what news to take back to his mother.

AT THE
OLD ROXY

"**I**t's nothing like you told Mum." Karen would have said more, but Tracey had already unlocked the front door and vanished into the dark hallway.

Karen stepped carefully across the sagging boards of the veranda, afraid that they'd splinter and collapse under her feet.

The only good thing she could find to say about the inside of the house was that it was cool after the blinding heat outside. There were several tiny rooms with peeling wallpaper and broken furniture, and then the depressing kitchen, with most of its inside wall missing so only the outer boards of the house showed. Tracey was filling a kettle at a sink that looked like a concrete washtub.

"You told Mum it was all fixed up. You said it was like a country cottage with climbing roses and a patio and a barbecue."

"Well, it will be! I can't do it all at once."

Karen looked for somewhere to sit down. Both chairs were piled with pots of paint, saws and hammers. She pushed two paper bags of nails and a roll of sandpaper back from the edge of the table and perched there, but the table tilted alarmingly and she sprang upright again.

Tracey spooned tea-leaves into a brown teapot. "Pretty soon I'm going to cut right through that wall there, and I'll have big glass doors opening on to the back garden. It'll be fantastic."

Karen peered through a gap between the boards. The back garden was wild, with knee-high weeds and one big tree. Under the tree was a small wooden building. Her heart sank. "Don't tell me that's the dunny," she said faintly.

"Of course not! There's a proper one in the bathroom." Tracey started shifting the things from the chairs on to the already loaded table. "I really need more bench space, cupboards and things. Still, can't have everything at once."

Karen eyed her sister sourly and thought that there were lots of things she really needed. The ugly brown lino on the floor curled at every join and the fridge looked prehistoric.

Tracey handed her a mug of tea. "We'll sit down for a minute, then I'll show you around. I'll give you a guided tour of my palace."

* * *

Later that night Karen lay awake in the room at the front of the house that was to be her bedroom. Her bed was a narrow mattress on the floor. There was a steel bar balanced across the corner of the room to hang things on. There were no drawers or dressing-table, and when Karen pointed this out, Tracey handed her a bundle of wire coathangers and told her it was best to hang everything up. Well, you could hardly hang up knickers and things, and whoever heard of hanging up jeans? So Karen left most of her stuff in her suitcase.

Tracey had left the hallway light on in case Karen had to get up during the night. It cast a dim glow into her room. Karen started to get up to shut the door, but she saw out of the corner of her eye a movement on the wall. She froze, half sitting up. It was something large and black. Suddenly it scuttled across the wall and paused near the window. Karen screamed.

Tracey appeared at the doorway and switched on the light. Karen was still crouched, half out of bed, pointing wordlessly at the huge spider. It was bigger than a saucer.

"It's only a huntsman. They're harmless."

"Kill it," said Karen through lips that would hardly move from fear.

"Don't be silly. It's beautiful. I'll shift it outside for you if you like." Tracey disappeared for a moment, and returned with a broom, a preserving jar and a cardboard folder. Gently she brushed the spider to the floor with the broom and placed the jar over it. The spider clung to the inside of the glass. She slid the folder under the jar and picked it up, holding the folder firmly beneath. "Look, Karen, see how pretty she is?"

Karen saw the shiny hairiness of it, glimpsed the ugly face before it shot up the glass inside Tracey's encircling hand. She shuddered. "Take it away."

Still Karen couldn't sleep. She left the bedroom light on, and lay for hours straining her eyes into the corners of the room, the large gaps where wall met wall and wall met floor and ceiling. She was glad she hadn't unpacked properly.

She was woken by the sound of hammering, then some sawing, then more hammering. She buried her head in her doona and dozed until she was woken by the noise of Tracey's ute, its starter motor straining raucously. At last it caught, and after a lot of revving the ute drove off. Thoroughly awake now, Karen jumped out of bed and made for the phone in the kitchen. Tracey wouldn't notice another long-distance call on her bill; she was always phoning Mum. In a moment Karen was talking to her friend Lynelle.

"It's ghastly. The house is falling down. The bathroom's a nightmare. My bedroom's full of monster spiders. Tracey's turned into this country freak who's only interested in sandpapering doorframes.

I'll be back, Lynelle, I'll be back in Melbourne before the end of the week."

But after she hung up, her depression settled again, because she knew she couldn't go back.

Karen was dressed by the time Tracey returned; she'd put on her short pink skirt and her cream lace bustier and she'd taken a lot of trouble with her hair, which wasn't easy in the dingy bathroom where the only mirror was dimmed by dark blotches. Tracey was lugging a machine like an old-fashioned floor polisher. "Oh, good, you're up," she called. "Can you give me a hand with this? It's a sander I've borrowed, but I can only have it for the morning. I'm going to rip up all the lino in the kitchen and do the floor. There's beautiful jarrah under all that — " She saw Karen, and paused for a moment. "Oh. You're not exactly dressed to help."

"I'm going down to the shops." At least, Karen thought, Tracey didn't go on about *that* being no way for a thirteen-year-old to dress, like Mum would have.

All Tracey said was, "They'll certainly notice you downtown, dressed like that. Still, before you go, can you help me shift the table? If you can without damaging your Madonna gear?"

It wasn't only the table that had to be moved through the door to the next room, it was every-thing that was on it, as well as the heavyweight fridge. Fortunately Tracey thought she could work around the gas stove. When Karen left, Tracey was tearing back the brittle lino and smashing it into pieces.

It took ten minutes to walk down the hill to the town centre, another ten minutes to walk up and down the boring shops on each side of the street. Karen saw nothing she wanted. Except food: there were plenty of takeaway places, and it was lunchtime; but she knew from experience that it was hard to lift things from a takeaway shop. She had no money. Mum had none to give her. Even the bus fare from Melbourne would have been impossible if Tracey hadn't sent a few dollars.

There was never any spare money. Christmas had been dismal, with Mum agonising about affording presents for the little ones. It was clear to Karen that there'd be nothing for her. She didn't care. She'd gone into the city and got her own presents at a couple of stores in Bourke Street Mall, right at lunchtime on Christmas Eve, when the customers were dozens deep and the shop assistants overworked — the skirt and bustier she was wearing for the first time today. Small things, soft fabric she could enclose in one hand like lightning and thrust into the pocket of her baggies, where they scarcely made a bulge.

She couldn't wear them on Christmas Day. Mum would have guessed. Anyway, why dress up for a day when you're forced to stick around an apartment in a highrise with the disappointed faces of little kids who'd been hoping for bikes and remote-control cars, and who only got packets of Smarties and the colouring books that were on special at Coles. But the dole seemed to have stretched to plenty of money for beer and vodka for *him*, Karen and Tracey's stepfather. By mid-afternoon his ho-ho-ho and tickles under the chin had turned to lurches and roaring. A terrific Christmas for me, she thought: hours spent barricaded in the baby's room, keeping out of his way, waiting for him to pass out.

The takeaway shop she was standing by wasn't busy. Karen wandered in and looked carefully at the selection of drinks. She went to the counter. "I was looking for lime-flavoured mineral water," she said. "Haven't you got any?"

The girl behind the counter sighed and went to the fridge herself, peering inside. "Should be some here," she said.

Karen slid a Violet Crumble into her bag from the boxes displayed on the counter. "Never mind. Maybe you've sold out. 'Bye."

A few shops further along, she sat on a seat outside the bank and ate the Violet Crumble. She had no idea what to do for the rest of the day. Tracey was right; people were staring at her. That was because she looked good, and every other female in this town got around in droopy trackpants or the sort of shapeless overalls that Tracey wore these days. It had been a shock for Karen to see her gorgeous older sister looking like a scarecrow at the bus station. She wasn't even twenty-two yet.

Across the road was a building with the high elaborate facade of an old-fashioned movie theatre, the name ROXY in big letters across the front. Karen decided to go across and see what kind of prehistoric movies they'd show in this town. Maybe that's how she could pass the afternoon. In the city she hadn't been able to perfect the knack of getting into the movies free, but here, in the country, they'd be easy to fool.

It wasn't a movie theatre at all, or any kind of theatre, not now. The Roxy was now a shop full of rows of the depressing tracksuits that everyone wore, sweatshirts with stupid slogans on the front, racks of facecloths and towels, shelves of blenders and alarm clocks and decanter sets. There was a makeup counter and boards hung with plastic earrings. Karen detached some earrings shaped like false teeth and put them in her bag. They'd do for a present to take home to Lynelle.

At the end of the shop was the stage, hidden by a gold velvet curtain. It was surrounded by swirls of moulded plaster picked out in pale blue and pink, shaded in charcoal by years of dust. Karen saw the boxes high at each side of the stage for rich people to sit in and be seen and envied, and behind her she saw the ornate balcony that concealed the upstairs seats.

There was a door beside the stage, marked STAFF ONLY. The store was empty apart from a woman at the counter far away by the street entrance. Silently Karen passed through the door.

The light was dim. There were piles of cartons and things in plastic wrappings, but beyond them was the stage — an enormous space behind the gold curtains, still and silent. She tiptoed to its centre. High above her were ropes dangling and ends of curtains that disappeared into a blackness so dense it was impossible to see where the roof was. At the side of the stage were tatters of black drapes. She walked through them, wrinkling her nose as the dust tickled, and then in the half light saw the gleam of a row of mirrors. She knew they should be surrounded by bright lightbulbs, and there should be the sound of excited voices, tenors singing up and down scales, the swirl of brilliant costumes, the smell of greasepaint. Now there was only this dusty silence. Not even a ghost.

Another passageway, some steps, and Karen was in a box looking over the stage. There was a velvet seat here, soft and wide as a curved sofa. Dust billowed as she sat down. The light from the shop below touched the row of grimy gilt Cupids that decorated the box. Maybe lovers used to sit here, deep in the shadows, or leaning out over the edge of the box so they could be seen — "Look at us! We're in love!" — watching men and women dancing and singing and acting love and pleasure and despair and anguish on the stage, a long time ago, back when the Cupids were clean and new.

It was so sad. No one would ever fix up the pretty things in this theatre. The Roxy would never have that kind of life again. It was being left to rot. It was a thing of the past that could never come back. Well, it happened, and you might as well accept it. Like Dad couldn't stop being dead and Karen would never again be the beloved baby of the family with one adored older sister.

It must have been the dust. Karen found tears running down her cheeks, and she gave a great gulp and for a while rested her head on her bare arms and let herself cry.

After a while she found a hardly used tissue in her shoulder-bag and scrubbed her eyes with it, and blew her nose. She left the soggy mess under the seat. Over the edge of the box she could see that the shop remained quiet. No one had noticed that she'd disappeared out the back entrance.

Then, from this height, Karen saw a stand she'd missed on her walk through the store. A tablecloth was displayed casually flung through a silver hoop. It was a glowing crimson, a circle of fabric with a fine pintucked border. Exactly what Tracey would like, nothing flowery, absolutely plain and elegant. It wouldn't be easy to get it out of the hoop without being seen, but they seemed to be half asleep in this shop anyway.

She slipped unseen through the STAFF ONLY door

into the shop, found the tablecloth and almost laughed aloud at how easy it was going to be. There was an identical tablecloth, folded neatly and wrapped in cellophane, in a stack beside the draped one. Other colours, too; blue, purple, pink and green. The red one was best, Karen thought, and her left hand delivered the shiny package to the depths of her bag while her right hand stroked the fabric draped from the ring.

But the half-asleep shop assistant stopped Karen as soon as she had two feet on the threshold of the street door, and she didn't even have time to think of running. Not that there were Bourke Street crowds to melt into. They found the false teeth earrings as well as the crimson tablecloth. The police car arrived in minutes. As she was bundled into the back seat and driven around the block to the cop shop, Karen closed her eyes. The faces on top of the daggy tracksuits were laughing.

She was put into a room with a table and two chairs and left on her own for a long time. Then the door opened and Tracey stood there.

"They've given you one more chance, Karen," Tracey said grimly as they climbed into the ute. "Your very last chance. We're so lucky they didn't check with the Melbourne cops."

Karen couldn't answer. It was so unfair that she'd been caught. They'd seemed completely dodo in that shop.

"I tried to warn you," Tracey was continuing. "I said they'd notice you. You were watched from the Violet Crumble onwards."

They were all spying on her. Definitely she couldn't live in this town. Karen clenched her jaw and stared out the ute window. Tracey wasn't driving directly back to her house. They went through some gates and drove among trees around the side of a hill.

"So," said Karen, "if I slopped around town in daggy old trackpants I could rob the bank and not be noticed?"

Tracey snorted and started laughing. She stopped the ute where they could see the town spilling beneath them down the hillside and over the valley. She reached over and hugged Karen's shoulders. "No. It's not that. You're a stranger in town, that's all. They're interested even though they'd never let on." She sighed. "A Violet Crumble and false teeth earrings I can understand. But a tablecloth?"

"It was for you," Karen mumbled. Her face was still nestled against Tracey's shoulder. "Something pretty for your house."

"Oh, Karen." Tracey sat upright. Her arm stopped hugging Karen and she gripped the steering-wheel with both hands. "I know you think the house is horrible. It probably is. But it's *mine*. It's not a poky apartment twenty floors up with a stepfather trying to grab a grope in every doorway." Karen shuddered and Tracey peered at her. "You, too? I'm not surprised. Well, I spent two years fruitpicking and saved every penny, and even then I only had enough for the deposit on the scruffiest broken-down hovel in the whole state."

Karen saw Tracey's fingers whiten as she held tightly to the steering-wheel. "I know it's awful, deep down I do," Tracey said. She started the engine. "I can't tell you how hurt I felt when I saw the look on your face when you arrived yesterday. But it was good for me to see you react like that, really. It forced me back to reality. My head's been full of how the house will look when it's finished. But of course I can't expect anyone else to live there." She started driving around the hill until they were back to the gates and on the road again. "I can find the money for your bus fare back to Melbourne."

Back to Melbourne. The hostile flat. She had no real place there either.

She glanced sideways at Tracey, surprised that she'd seen so clearly what Karen had thought about her house. Karen wished she hadn't made it so obvious. This was her idolised older sister, part of the past she'd been remembering in the old Roxy. Tracey wasn't one of the enemy.

The ute stopped at Tracey's house. Tracey led the way through the front door as she had yesterday. Karen followed, and then she saw a shiny brass key tied to her bedroom door handle.

"That's a new front door key I got cut for you,"

Tracey said. "I picked it up from the hardware when I took the sander back. Never mind, I can always use a spare key."

Beside the bedroom door was propped something like a broom, perhaps more like a floor mop with a plastic scoop and a lid at the end where the sponge should be. The paint on its long handle was new and glistening.

"It's a spider catcher," said Tracey. "I thought you might sleep easier if you had one. You can stand miles away and scoop them up and put them out the door. It doesn't hurt them at all."

Karen dumped her shoulder-bag on the floor beside her rumpled bed.

"Anyway," Tracey said, "come and see what I've done to the kitchen."

The table and the fridge were still outside the kitchen door, so Karen had to squeeze past to stand next to Tracey in the doorway.

"Don't step on it!" Tracey warned. "It's not dry yet."

The late afternoon sun slanted in from the window and lit the red-brown satiny wood floor that spread from corner to corner of the room. The kitchen was transformed. It was as if someone had polished the Cupids at the Roxy.

Karen looked around, noticed how the wallpaper clung roughly to mouldings on the walls and over the archway into the sitting-room. She wondered what treasures of decoration it was hiding. "We could tear the wallpaper off," she said.

"We could," said Tracey.

"Tear up all the old carpets — maybe all the floors are like that underneath."

"Maybe."

"Perhaps I'll stay on for a few days."

"If you like," said Tracey.

HOSTILITIES

It was four o'clock in the afternoon on the shortest day of the year.

"I suppose that's better than calling it the longest night of the year," said Marian.

Still afternoon, and yet the cars travelling towards them rushed out of the greyness with their headlights on, as though to warn that things were worse where they were coming from. Liz could believe it. The clouds hung low and misty on the hills; ahead they gathered in charcoal folds.

For some distance now the car had been trapped behind a mobile concrete mixer. Liz watched the rotating mouth of the huge urn until it seemed to fill her whole vision. The truck struggled on the hills and braked suddenly at sharp turns. The rainwater lying on the road fizzed in a fine oily spray on to the windscreen from the truck's back wheels.

Choking fumes from its exhaust seeped into the car. Liz was about to comment on this, but was glad she hadn't when Jasper in the back seat made an exaggerated spluttering noise followed by several groaning deep breaths as if he were dying. "My mother," he said then, the emphasis on *my*, "always passes trucks."

Liz looked at Marian to see if she'd been stung into a response. She hadn't. Her lips pressed together a trace more firmly, her long fingers curled a little further around the steering-wheel. It was only because Liz knew her mother so well that she saw these minute signs.

More hills and twists in the road. The rain started to fall steadily. The slowly spinning mouth of the concrete truck seemed to be forever hanging in front of the car. Liz wondered if it would fill up with rain until runny concrete sprayed out and covered them.

"Have you got our headlights on, Marian?" she heard Jasper say. *Our* headlights? What does he mean by *our*? It's Marian's car, not his. "There are heaps of cars behind us," he went on. "They've all got their headlights on."

Marian released the steering-wheel long enough to snap on the headlights. "The good thing about the shortest day," she said, "is that you know it can't get any worse. Every day after that is a little longer, a little closer to spring. You can't help feeling better, happier, somehow."

"My mother," said Jasper from the back, "says it's neurotic to get depressed in the winter."

At that moment an overtaking lane blossomed on the road ahead. The concrete truck seemed to shrink, as Marian flew the car past. Liz turned as they passed to peer at the truck driver, and as she did she saw from the corner of her eye Jasper gesturing through the back window. As he turned back he saw Liz watching him, and he squinted his eyes at her.

The car was singing along now. The rain lessened to a fine drizzle and the sky lightened as if some late sunshine might break through. It was understandable, Liz was thinking as she watched for a rainbow, that her mother should fall in love. She'd been prepared for it to happen sooner or later, and when it had happened it was less of a trial than she'd expected. The man was nice. His only drawback was his son, Jasper.

"Do your best to get on with Jasper," her mother had said, predictably enough. "When Jack and I get married he'll be living with us all, for some of the time anyway."

Before she met him, Liz thought that Jasper would be interesting. She looked up his name in a baby-naming book and found that it meant "the keeper of the treasure." He didn't measure up to his name. He called her mother "Marian."

"If he's going to call you Marian, so am I," she told her mother, expecting an argument.

"Of course," Marian replied immediately.

His birthday was exactly the same day as hers. They both turned twelve within an hour of each other. That was ten months ago. He and his father were staying with them. She had to share her birthday.

They were past the hilly part of their journey. The narrow road across the plains stretched ahead and disappeared into mistiness beyond the reach of the headlights. It was nearly dark. The inside of the car became bright from the lights of a vehicle gaining on them from behind.

"Good heavens, it's that concrete truck," Marian said. "It must have found a new lease on life."

It drew very close behind. It was about to drive over the car.

"What's it trying to do? I'm not going to go faster in this weather." Marian sounded less cool than usual.

"It wants to overtake," said Jasper.

Marian sidled the car close to the edge of the sealed surface. The truck didn't pass. It stayed there, its lights glaring.

Liz said, "It's because of Jasper. He gave the finger to the driver out of the back window when we overtook."

"I did not," Jasper said instantly.

"I hope you didn't," Marian said in a level voice. "I don't want to deal with aggressive truck drivers."

"Perhaps he won't pass because the road's too

narrow. Can we stop?" Liz tried to keep her voice as level as Marian's.

"I don't think stopping's a good idea. Besides, look how boggy it is at the edge of the seal." Marian was gradually slowing the car. She was leaning forward to see against the shine of the truck's headlights in the rearvision mirror. The truck behind roared as the driver dropped down through the gears to match the car's speed.

"There's a turn-off ahead! I can see the road sign!" Liz grabbed Marian's arm and pointed.

Marian flicked on the indicator and slowed further to make the turn. Behind them the truck slowed too.

"His indicator's on, too," Jasper said.

Unbelievably, the truck turned after them. This road was narrower, rough and unsealed. The car slithered on its surface.

"Keep a watch for some lights, a farmhouse, anything," Marian said. Her hands were clenched on the wheel, fighting to control the car. Liz saw her face, flour-white in the glare from behind.

There weren't any farmhouses, or none with lights strong enough to shine as far as the road. "I'm not stopping," Marian said. "I will not."

And then, slowly, the brightness in the car lessened. Liz turned to look out the back window. "I think the truck's stopped," she said. "Perhaps it will turn around."

"Keep watching," Marian said, although Liz saw

her glancing from the road to the rearvision mirror. "Make sure it does turn round."

The truck's lights grew fainter, and then disappeared. "It's gone," Liz said quietly.

Marian stopped the car. She leaned her arms on the steering-wheel and rested her forehead on them. After a moment she looked up. "Well. Where the hell are we, do you think?"

The blackness outside pressed against the side windows and swallowed the beams from the headlights. "If we turn round," Liz said, "we're sure to get to the road we were on before."

"What if," Jasper said, "that truck didn't turn around? What if it's still there, waiting for us?"

Marian laughed a little. "Well, there's no point keeping on in this direction. We might run out of petrol before we get to where this road's going."

"We're short of *petrol*?" Jasper said. The scorn rolled like a wave from the back seat.

Cautiously, in short backward and forward runs with the engine racing, Marian turned the car on the narrow road. "I can't even remember how far along this road we came," she said quietly to Liz. There was an unmistakable sigh from the back.

"It doesn't matter," Liz said. "We can't get lost." But she was leaning forward, scanning the darkness ahead until her eyes hurt.

And there it was, the concrete truck. Its cab was empty, its lights extinguished. It was nearly blocking the road.

Liz closed her eyes as the car slowed almost to a walk and Marian squeezed it past the truck. She felt the swing of the car as the wheels slid in the mud. Then the car gathered speed again, and Liz opened her eyes. Marian was smiling. Liz wanted to cheer. But still the road kept coming endlessly under the lights.

That was when the engine acted strangely. It faltered, then surged ahead again. Another falter, and it stopped. "Petrol," Marian said.

The rain tapped against the car roof. After a moment Marian turned off the headlights. There was utter blackness.

Nobody spoke for some time. A point of light, furred by the rain, moved slowly from left to right across the windscreen. It was impossible to judge its distance. It could have been someone with a torch crossing the road in front of the car.

"That might be a car going along the main road we were on before," Marian said. In a moment another blur of light crossed in the other direction.

"How far away do you think that road is?" Liz asked.

"Don't know. It might be just a short walk but it's hard to tell. Anyway, let's go." Marian took the keys out of the ignition and buttoned her jacket. Liz considered protesting about the rain, the dark and the coldness outside the car, but then Jasper said, "We're going to *walk*?" in a horrified voice so she said, "Of course, Jasper, we can't sit here all night, can we?" She got out of the car, steadying herself as her feet slithered on the muddy ground.

Marian found a torch under the front seat. She checked that the car doors were locked. "OK. Let's go," she said again.

They walked as fast as they could on the slippery road. Seven sets of lights crossed through the darkness beyond them. But they never seemed to be getting closer. "I'm sure I can hear a car engine," Liz said.

"You can," Jasper said. "But it's coming from behind us." They were lit suddenly by headlights turned on full. Even though their eyes were dazzled, the shape of the concrete truck was clearly defined.

"Stick together, hold hands, right over at the side of the road," Marian ordered. "Keep walking. Don't look back."

The truck slowed to match their pace. In a low gear it roared and spat fumes like a pursuing dragon. "Don't run," Marian snarled as Liz tugged at her hand to move faster.

At last with a monstrous trumpeting from its horn the truck swerved and rushed past. Its back wheels danced and flung rivers of mud back at them. The truck's tail lights flared, then its noise slowly diminished until it vanished.

They stood until they saw the glow of its headlights appear on what they knew was the sealed road ahead. They watched the glow move across the darkness and disappear in the distance.

They trudged on. With her wet sleeve Liz wiped the mud that had splattered across her face.

"So what do we do when we get to the road?" Jasper asked.

"We need petrol, a phone. Either or both," Marian replied.

"So we hitch-hike," Jasper stated.

"Perhaps. I don't know. Maybe." Marian's voice was unsteady.

"Hitch-hiking is asking for trouble, my mother says," Jasper said.

"Will you *shut up* about your mother." Liz faced Jasper. She saw the streaks and splashes of mud on his face. "I'm sick to death of hearing about your mother. She's no use to us now so just shut up!" Liz's rage made her words jumble.

"Well, what use is *your* mother?" Jasper replied calmly. "The car's stuck up a country road with no petrol and we're soaking and covered in mud and on an expedition to who knows where. And she hasn't really got a clue what to do next."

"We wouldn't even be here if we didn't have to deliver you to *your* precious mother. So just shut up or I'll push you under this mud and leave you here." Liz's threat was realistic because she was bigger than Jasper. Marian had left them, walking ahead with the torch, so Liz couldn't see Jasper's face any more. But the stillness of his outline, his silence, spelt to her an open declaration of war. Yes, she conveyed back to him in her silence, it's war.

Liz liked history. That is, she disliked it less than she disliked other school subjects. It was a class session when the time didn't drag. She considered what it was like to be a horse in the American Civil War. And wondered who fed the horses. And who grew the crops to feed the horses.

Then there were the phrases that began these wonderings. "Hostilities commenced on 14 August 1861." "War was declared after the incident at Sarajevo in 1914." They reminded her of the night of the shortest day, the nightmarish car trip that marked the beginning of hostilities between herself and Jasper.

At first it was a war with no fighting, because Jasper was staying at his mother's place. But two months later he was back living with Marian and Jack and Liz in their brand-new house. He arrived two days before their thirteenth birthday.

"We'll have a party for you both," Jack and Marian told Liz. "Invite your friends so Jasper can meet some people here."

Liz didn't invite anybody and pretended that nobody wanted to come. She knew her mother was hurt when the afternoon arrived and there were just the four of them, staring at each other. Liz didn't care. The night before, she found the evidence that proved hostilities had begun. Jasper had been in the house only one day and he'd invaded her territory.

She'd felt a painful stab in her arm a minute after putting on her shirt. She ripped off her shirt and in the mirror saw the earwig, its shiny body arched like a scorpion's, the mean pincers at its tail sinking into the tender flesh near her armpit. She stifled a shriek and flicked the creature off. She looked in the wardrobe and saw all its mates. They knew she was looking. They arched themselves and their pincers waved at her skin.

Obviously, Liz thought, it was Jasper who had put the infestation in her wardrobe. She locked her room after that, and carried the key in her pocket.

Jasper, for his thirteenth birthday, was given a spaniel puppy. He named him Wolfgang.

Liz bided her time, planned her plans, and passed the hours by subverting Wolfgang. Chocolate biscuits were Wolfgang's greatest weakness. Liz kept a supply hidden and fed them to Wolfgang when no one was looking. Sometimes Wolfgang would go to Jasper when he called, but it was Liz he really loved. He flung himself at Liz whenever he saw her, whether she called him or not.

Because he was Jasper's dog, it was Jasper who had to clean up the chocolatey vomit Wolfgang left in every room. He did the cleaning up very cheerfully. He was besotted with the little dog. But the damage was done: Wolfgang preferred Liz to Jasper and made it clear.

In any sort of war Liz knew it was essential to know the enemy well. Jasper left two letters addressed and sealed for Marian to post when she drove into town. Liz took them to her bedroom and locked the door.

She opened the letter to Jasper's mother first. Most of the letter was about his birthday present, Wolfgang. Liz skimmed through until she found her own name. "Liz is being very nice to Wolfgang which is kind of her. She still doesn't seem to like me much although I'm trying to be nice to her."

Cunning liar, Liz thought.

The other letter had only a few words in the centre of the page. "Suzie, I'm missing you." A girl-friend, Liz thought. I wonder if he lies to her as he does to his mother?

Liz found she could stick back together the envelope addressed to Jasper's mother so it didn't look tampered with. But not the letter to the girl-friend. Liz tore that letter and its envelope into a hundred pieces.

She opened Jasper's bedroom door and went in, moving silently even though she knew Jasper was away somewhere with Jack. A faint new-house smell still lingered in the corners. The room was bare of anything that could be distinctively Jasper. There was nothing in the desk drawer except a felt pen and a few sheets of the paper she knew he used for letters. There were two novels she recognised from the sitting-room shelves on the table by his bed. A pale blue windbreaker hung tidily on the back of the chair. There was no scope here for Liz to make a major offensive in the war.

Outside the heavy earthmoving machinery roared as it prepared the ground for a house to be built next door. The noise and the faint tremors in the earth filtered into the room where Liz moved stealthily. It was like being close to the front. Liz removed the cap from the felt pen and placed the pen point down in the windbreaker's chest pocket.

In the early evening Liz sat on a plank left by the builders and watched Marian planting silver birches on the edge of the patch of earth that would one day soon be a lawn. Liz was plotting, only half listening to Marian. Marian wanted to talk about Jasper.

"He and I had a long talk this afternoon. He's quite a nice kid, really. I know you thought he was a pain on the night of the dreaded concrete truck, but you've got on OK since then, haven't you, Liz?"

Liz didn't answer. She was thinking about Jasper's efforts to get all the adults on to his side.

Marian gave a little shriek and whacked at the ground with her spade. "This place is infested with creepies," she said. "I found earwigs in my shoes this morning. Right inside the wardrobe."

This development surprised Liz. It seemed a stupid move for Jasper to make, but then, maybe it was really a clever step in his overall campaign against her. If Liz's room alone was attacked, his campaign might be too obvious.

That night as they all sat around the dinner table Jasper's eyes seemed to glitter. Liz couldn't eat.

She was woken in the morning by Jack and Marian's cheery "See you later!" as they left for their early-morning jog. The front door slammed, and the sound of their footsteps faded. Liz lay in bed for a few moments, strangely light-headed, a little excited, as if she knew that today something had to happen.

Then she heard a thundering and felt the house vibrate. Through a gap in the curtains she saw a truck with a mobile concrete mixer lumbering into position among the excavations on the land next door. At the edge of the square cut into the bare earth the truck stopped reversing. The huge urn shook. A tide of liquid concrete fell into the hole and flowed to each corner. It would become the floor of the basement of the house. Now it bubbled and moved like a thick grey soup.

Suddenly Liz flew out of her bedroom into the hallway. She shouted in a voice high with hysteria. "Jasper! Jasper! Wolfgang's stuck in the wet concrete!"

There was silence for a moment, then the crashing of Jasper's frantic running across the wooden kitchen floor, out of the back door, past the side of the house to the building site. Again at her window, Liz glimpsed his anguished face as his head twisted from side to side, searching.

But he didn't jump into the ankle-deep grey slush, as Liz had hoped. She watched in astonishment as he climbed hand over hand up to the huge concrete-filled urn.

Why didn't he stop to wonder how tiny Wolfgang could possibly jump up there? Anyway, Wolfgang was nowhere near the wet concrete, or the concrete mixer either, as Liz knew well. He was lying at her feet, chewing the rug.

Then Liz saw the driver in the cab of the concrete truck. For an exhilarating moment she was sure he was the driver from that night two months ago.

The truck's engine started with a roar louder than the trundling machinery of the revolving urn.

The truck reversed in two jerky movements towards the square cut into the earth, ready to pour the second layer of concrete. Liz saw Jasper clinging desperately, but he couldn't hold on strongly enough. He was flung off, and landed on his back in the first layer of slushy concrete.

The driver was unaware. Liz screamed and the little dog at her feet stopped chewing and trembled.

The urn tilted, and a river of grey concrete ran on to Jasper's struggling figure.

For an instant of time, the tiny fraction of a second that it takes for a thought to flash into being, Liz held the balance between Jasper's life and death.

She sped outside, knowing she would be in time to rescue Jasper. She was screaming and sobbing in a total frenzy. But in her heart she was calm and triumphant. She knew this was the finest moment in her campaign.

She was saving his life. From this moment, Jasper would have to be grateful to her for as long as he lived.

LIES

Raymond Reginald Moore's bedroom window was shaded by the grapevine that covered the narrow veranda every summer.

Green light drifted in one Tuesday morning at ten past five and opened his eyes. It was summer, but so early that the room was cool and his bed had a soft smooth warmth.

He could see a small movement in the filtered light at the window, a beetle, maybe a spider, slowly moving downwards. He hoped it was outside the glass. Raymond preferred that things with eight or six legs stayed on the other side of the walls and windows of the bedroom, but this was a feeling he kept hidden from the others. There were a lot of feelings best kept from the rest of the family when you were the youngest.

The moving creature vanished behind a large

vine leaf. *Outside* the window, it was, Raymond knew then.

The pale cliffs across the river — Raymond could see glimpses of these through the crowding leaves — took on a pinkness as the new sun touched them. People still called it a river, even at this time of the year when it was hardly more than a scatter of stagnant ponds.

At nine o'clock, nearly four hours away, Raymond's mother was taking him to the doctor. It was for his cough, she said, or maybe his sinuses or hay fever; but Raymond knew what it was really for.

The spider was still hidden. It was probably spinning a net to catch its breakfast between the leaves.

His mother would have discussed with the doctor the thing she didn't discuss with Raymond any more. Raymond shifted sideways a little. Of course, as usual, the warm cocoon of his bed had been deceptive. Further from his body it was cool and damp. As he moved his leg he heard the crackle of the plastic undersheet.

He left his bed and pulled away the doona, peeled off the sheet, all silently so Derek wouldn't wake. Gently he opened the outer door to the veranda. It creaked and Raymond froze but Derek didn't move. Derek's head was covered and there was no sign that he was breathing. Raymond wondered if he was dead.

He stopped by the vine leaves on the veranda to

check the spider, but couldn't see it. As he turned away, the corner of his eye caught the same movement, the same black creature moving cautiously, hesitantly, on the cliffs whose pinkness was turning to gold as the sun grew stronger. It was a man climbing down the cliffs towards the riverbed. A trick of his eyes, a lie told by light and distance, Raymond realized, had turned a grown man into an insect at his window.

Raymond walked around the side of the house, every few steps turning his head to watch the climber, half expecting him to fall, until the corner of the house blocked his view and he entered the side door that opened into the porch with the washing machine in it. He threw the bundled sheet into the machine, then took off his underpants and dropped the lid on them too.

He dressed in fresh clothes crisp and warm from the shelves in the cupboard beside the hot water heater. Then he left the house.

From the veranda with the grapevine the land fell steadily to the riverbed. It took two or three minutes if you ran, twenty seconds if you were sitting on a flattened cardboard box when the grass was long and dry. Here the riverbed was wide and flat, a stretch of sand and fine gravel. There were some pools you could step over, and in the centre a slow-moving stream full of blobs of cream-brown scum.

That was what it was like in summer, the time

of the year when you needed a big deep river to cool off in. In winter, the river swelled from scummy ponds to an ugly brown torrent carrying branches, tree trunks, car bodies, and upturned swollen drowned cows.

In the winter floods two years ago, the river had overflowed its banks and climbed the grass to the veranda of Raymond's house. His mother, and Derek his brother, and his two older sisters — but not his father, who was still in prison — had been evacuated to the Public Library during the night, carrying their doonas and pillows, along with three other families whose houses were close to the river. Raymond had stayed awake all night. He wasn't afraid of the flood reaching them — the library was on the hill near the church and the Shire offices — but he'd heard Derek's joke to his sisters, a stupid joke about Raymond flooding himself wherever he slept, said in a voice just loud enough for Raymond to hear.

Now, as Raymond crossed the riverbed, he saw the man again; only for a brief moment, because the figure fell flat in a single movement behind a bush poised on the cliff edge.

Raymond knew all the shelves and trails and dangerous slips that made up the cliffs along this part of the river and for as far as you could see in either direction. The man had been heading along a dead-end ledge. Raymond crossed the rest of the riverbed, and started to climb the secret track up the cliff face. Finally he reached the crouching man who, believing himself hidden, was peering through the branches of the bush, down to the riverbed.

"Why are you hiding?" Raymond asked curiously.

The man drew in a great gust of breath and sprang to face Raymond, still crouching but with his fingers spread out in a position of attack. Raymond flinched as if he was going to be hit. The man relaxed his arms a little. He remained crouched, though, ready to spring at an instant's warning. He wasn't young, somewhere between twenty and thirty, Raymond guessed. His clothes weren't as black as they'd looked against the pale earth of the cliffs; he wore a faded navy-blue shirt and jeans. He hadn't shaved for a bit and there was dark stubble on his chin and around his jaw. His eyes had purple shadows under them, and they were opened so wide that the whites seemed to surround the pupils.

"Why are you sneaking around here?" he said at last.

"I'm not. I saw you climbing down from the top of the cliff. You came down the hard way."

"Did I?" The man straightened a little and at the same time seemed to relax. He glanced around, back down to the riverbed, a quick look along the cliff above. "You're on your own?"

Raymond kept his eyes on the man, and made a sideways movement with his chin. "I live down there."

"I was trying to get to the river before sunrise. I need a drink. Some water."

"You can't drink that water."

"No?" The man looked at Raymond's face, which was screwed up in disgust.

"You'd die. It's full of poison. There's a factory upstream that chucks all their rubbish in the river. They reckon they don't but there's never any fish in there."

The man was sitting on the narrow ledge now, his forearms resting on his knees, staring down at the river with so many faults. "I don't suppose," he said slowly, "I don't suppose you could get me some water to drink from somewhere else? From your place maybe? And something to eat?"

"Are you hungry? You could come home for breakfast — " Raymond stopped talking and considered what he'd said and wondered why he'd said it. Nobody would bring a stranger to a meal at his house, least of all Raymond.

"Breakfast? Sounds agreeable. Very agreeable indeed. What's on the menu at your place this morning? Orange juice, bacon and eggs? Sausages? Fresh coffee?"

"No," Raymond replied, nervous now. "Just toast and a cup of tea."

"Sounds pretty good to me. Well, you're a good kid to ask but I'm not into accepting invites to breakfast just now. So. Why don't you run along and get me some water, and bring it back to me here. Our secret, OK?"

"Why's it a secret?"

The man explained that he and some mates were playing a war game, and while it wasn't cheating if Raymond secretly brought him some water, it would definitely be against the rules for the man to go into a store and buy a strawberry milkshake and a pie; and anyway, he didn't have any money on him. That was also part of the rules.

Raymond returned to the house, stealthily, thinking carefully. It was a few minutes after six o'clock when he filled a plastic drink bottle with tap water, and took four slices from the bag of toast bread. Any more than four slices would be noticed.

Raymond was thinking about his uncle who lived in Victoria and who was one of a group that played war games. They crept through the bush and shot each other with blotches of red paint. They dressed like soldiers, in boots and army camouflage gear. They didn't look at all like that man on the cliffs. Perhaps, Raymond thought, he was playing a different kind of war game.

Nobody saw him leave the house. "They were all still asleep," Raymond told the man, who then said, "Bread and water," in an amused sort of voice before unscrewing the cap of the plastic bottle and tipping it up to drink.

"I put honey on the bread, but that's all. I think we've run out of margarine."

The man didn't answer. He was eating the honey sandwiches in huge bites.

"You don't look like you're one of those war game people," said Raymond.

"You're going to have to forget you saw me," the man said when the bread was all gone. "I want to make that clear. Do you understand?"

Then he told Raymond that he'd made a break from gaol, a reasonable thing to do, the only possible thing, he said, when a man was unjustly convicted, and put behind bars for a crime he didn't do.

Raymond didn't answer for a while. He was thinking about his father. "I know what you mean," he told the man. "My dad did twenty months in gaol for something he didn't do. They reckoned he was doing up stolen cars. But he told me he wasn't. He was framed. He was set up. Is that what happened to you?"

The man nodded slowly. "Something like that," he said.

"I wish my dad had escaped. Then maybe people would've realised he shouldn't have been put in gaol in the first place."

"It doesn't work quite like that," the man said, but Raymond was hardly listening. He had decided to help this man with his escape. It would be a way of telling his father that he understood.

* * *

Raymond Reginald Moore was afraid of his father and he wished he wasn't because his fear made him tongue-tied and he wanted his father to know how much he admired him.

Raymond's father was gaoled on Raymond's eighth birthday, released nearly two years later. He was a changed man; everyone said that. In the time of his imprisonment the service station that had employed him went out of business, and the other service station in town didn't want to give him a job when he came out of gaol. For a year now Raymond's father had been unemployed. Sometimes he had beer for breakfast. He never got over being a changed man. He showed no signs of changing back.

Raymond's sisters and brother avoided Dad as much as possible, so Raymond did the same, but he felt he was the only one in the family who realised how terrible it was to be imprisoned wrongfully. It was no problem to keep out of Dad's way. He was asleep until after the kids left for school, and he was at the pub after school and far into the night. When Raymond did see his father, the words he wanted to say were dried in his mouth by his awkwardness.

But that morning, when Raymond came back from the cliffs, he found his father standing in the kitchen, stony-faced. Raymond saw that in his haste he'd left the bread and the open jar of honey on the kitchen table, and black streams of ants overran everything.

"The one morning in my life I try to get some breakfast in this house I find that some clown's donated it to the ant population."

Raymond picked up the plastic bag of sliced bread and tried to shake the ants off, but he'd dribbled strands of honey from the knife over the bread and the ants wouldn't leave. They ran along his fingers, and he tried uselessly to brush them off, miserable, knowing he'd failed again.

His father took the change jar from the top of the fridge and emptied the coins on to the bench. There weren't many. He counted out two dollars in five and ten cent pieces. "I'll get a pie at the store," he said.

Raymond drew in a deep breath. He wanted to tell his father right now.

"Dad — " he started, then coughed because his voice sounded squeaky. His father stopped, his hand on the doorknob. "There's a man on the cliffs. He's escaped from prison!"

Raymond's father faced him, a satisfied smile on his face. "A runner, eh?" he said.

Raymond felt encouraged. "So I took him some breakfast, and showed him where he could hide. He's not meant to be in prison. He didn't do what they said he did. He said he was unjustly convicted."

His father laughed. "They all say that. Every bloke that's inside says that. Can you blame them?"

Raymond was too shocked to answer.

"So what's he supposed to have done?" his father continued. "This *innocent* bloke?"

"Don't know."

"Oh well, it doesn't matter. There'll be some sort of reward on his head. And even if there isn't, this town'll have to change its snooty attitude if I lead the police to a wanted man. What d'ya reckon, son?" He laughed again and patted Raymond's head. "You're a good chap for letting me know about him."

Raymond was in misery. His father had completely misunderstood.

"So where is he exactly, son? You said you showed him where to hide."

Raymond stared at the floor. He couldn't speak. His father grabbed his upper arms and shook him roughly. "Where is he? Stupid little prick — don't you understand what *reward* means?"

All Raymond's words burst out now. "He didn't do it. He was framed, Dad, just like you were. What if you'd escaped, and someone had dobbed you in? You know it's not fair to be shut away for something you didn't do!"

His father dropped Raymond's arms. "Still up on the cliffs, isn't he. Hiding in the cave till night time. Waiting for you to bring him a torch and as much food as you can rip off from round here." He fixed his eyes on Raymond's. "I'm right, aren't I? *Tell me!*"

"It isn't fair," Raymond mumbled. His father had guessed. "Why don't you let him get away?"

"What would you know about anything?" Dad was looking pleased. "You don't even know how to stop pissing the bed."

His father was gone, slamming the back door. Then it swung open again, and Raymond heard, "Tell your mother I don't know when I'll be back, but when I am, we'll be rich."

Without letting himself think too much, Raymond did what he was supposed to do every morning before school. He collected a sheet from the jumble of washed sheets in the cupboard by the washing machine. He was carrying it up the passage to his bedroom when his mother called to him from the bathroom.

"Don't forget we're going to the doctor's this morning! I'll give Derek a note to take to school to explain why you're late."

Raymond continued to the bedroom he shared with Derek, who couldn't have been dead because now he was kneeling on the floor, burrowing in a drawer in search of socks.

They ignored each other. Raymond saw that the plastic undersheet was dry now. He looked out of the window through the vine leaves at the cliff, almost white in the hot sun. The escaped prisoner had said he'd hide in the cave until nightfall, but that could just be another lie in Raymond's life. Perhaps he was well on the way to Sydney by now, and Dad wouldn't find him.

Raymond tore off the uncomfortable crackling plastic sheet and kicked it under the bed. He smoothed the sheet over the foam rubber mattress and took a lot of trouble to tuck in all the sides, to fold the covers under neatly.

He went back to the kitchen and made himself a cup of tea with a teabag. "I'm not going to the doctor's," he said to his mother. "So you don't need to worry about giving Derek a note."

"But Raymond love, what about your — your hay fever?"

"I think it's cured itself. It's not going to happen any more," Raymond said. "It's really the way I used to wet the bed every night we're talking about, isn't it? Well, it's not going to happen any more."

Raymond didn't pass on his father's message about arriving home rich. He simply didn't believe it.

I SAW MY NAME
IN A BOOK

Solana crossed the bridge with cautious steps. She tested each board before she let it take her weight. Its wood was black with rain, encrusted with green and orange moss. The handrails were rotting and in some places gone completely: fallen into the boiling red water below, to be worried and tumbled until they crumbled to leaden waterlogged pieces and sank.

Three more steps — two; a jump and Solana's feet found the solid ground. For a moment she looked down to the red water rushing through the ravine. Heavy steam hung like a pall over the saturated ground on the other side as it dried in the fierce sunlight. She kicked at the boards at her end of the bridge. With a sigh and a creak or two they slewed sideways, then slithered out of sight. The whole bridge shivered. The rolling planks parted *and fell downwards to where the water received them with hardly a splash.*

Stupid book. I close it with a slap and it spins across the table and drops to the floor.

That bridge took more than a kick to dislodge. It took me an hour to find a branch strong enough to use as a crowbar. Another hour went in exhausting efforts to lever the rotten wood free of the bolts, all the time panicking that the hunters on my heels would get to the bridge before I'd dealt with it. A couple of kicks! Not true. It sounds so easy. Like I had some kind of magic on my side.

I've found a derelict hut, a cabin that might have been used in the past by bushwalkers. It has bunks against one wall, two rubber mattresses covered in a murky blue fabric with faded stars and spaceships. A fireplace dominates one end wall. The woodbox is empty. It's impossible to have a fire, anyway; the smoke would give me away.

I'm very thirsty. There's a sink, but of course the taps don't work, nor do the shower taps in an alcove behind a curtain — more stars and spaceships. And there's this shelf with these old books.

The cabin becomes shadowy. Rain clouds are moving across again, cutting out the sunlight.

Under the sink there are two tin bowls. I flick away the dust and dead spiders with the end of the curtain and take them outside as the freezing rain starts to fall. For a moment or two I lift my face upwards, mouth open, tongue out to collect some of the drops.

They knew about the desert and thought no escapee could survive the dryness. I drank all the water I had with me on the first day — yesterday. But then started this crazy unseasonal pattern of rain, sun, rain — heat followed by cold. No one predicted this weather, but here it is, and it's exactly described in this book. Too cold to be outside in the freezing rainstorms, it says. Too hot to move in the sun.

With the bridge smashed I feel safe, for a while. Finding this cabin was like finding an extra present under the Christmas tree. I can rest.

The rainstorm has passed. The tin bowls have collected an impressive amount of water.

Solana turned from the crevasse, faced her future-land. The past-land lay behind her, cut away by the dropping of the bridge, and already it was shrouded in mist. Ahead the sand and rocks glittered in the sunlight.

And crouching in a grove of olive trees was a cottage, its door ajar, its windows glinting as if lit by welcoming fires within.

I can't read any more. I'm too tired, and anyway the light's fading. The real sun has touched the real horizon and dusk has fallen. Some rules still hold.

* * *

It's morning. I drink some water, looking through the door across the desert to the east, knowing I don't know what to do next.

Solana knew how much depended upon her staying alive. The safety of the whole tribe —

I suppose it depends what you call a tribe. There's my father with his pointed bald head wearing his spare glasses, the ones that make him look like a moron, because his others have been broken and there's nowhere to get them fixed now that the fighting's started. There's my mother with her careful voice and her honey-grey hair escaping in wisps from the knot on the back of her head. She's wearing a red cotton dress with green and yellow parrots around the hem of its skirt. I hope she's not cold. Perhaps someone will lend her a jacket. But then maybe these bands of coldness aren't travelling as far as the city.

When the banging came on the door, my father whispered to me: "Right, Solana, you know what to do. Wait till everyone's gone, then bugger off as fast as you can"; and I couldn't help glancing at my mother, expecting her usual protest when my father uses what she calls yobbo language, but her face was white and still, her whole body tensed towards the door which would burst inwards in a matter of seconds.

At yobbo language times she threatens to send me back east to her old school where the girls have perfect pleats and elegant diction. So far my father has resisted this. It's a relief.

After the city was invaded, during the days when nothing seemed to happen — apart from the furtive night-time meetings at our place, the phone calls with odd messages about owls or plagues of rats, the flashes of light from the barn after midnight — during those days my father made me memorise the way to the camel trail, an unused and forgotten track leading across the desert to the border. We knew that the main road to the east was blocked by enemy troops. He made me practise driving the old farm truck, the one with the sticky clutch. He filled water containers, topped up the petrol, snarled at me when I let the motor stall in sand-drifts on these practice runs.

One day the coded phone messages stopped. The phone was dead. Then there was no power, no water from the taps; and we learned later that day that it was the same everywhere.

That night the real fighting started. I could see the flashes of explosions far away over the city, a few moments later hear the crashes. I was alone. I didn't know if my mother and father would come home safely.

They did, a little before dawn, my mother driving the station wagon through the dark with the headlights off, my father blinking with his broken glasses in his left hand, his right hand holding a wad of blood-soaked tissues to his temple.

It was after breakfast that we saw the line of dust rising along the road from the city, heading for our house. Breakfast had been tin-tasting tea made from the dregs in the rainwater tank, and bacon cooked in a wok balanced on the fire. It was like camping. It would have been fun but for the tension.

The convoy stopped outside the house in a swirl of dust, brakes screeching. "Three jeeps just to arrest two people," my father said in a disgusted voice. There was the banging on the door. Then he gave me the ungentle shove between the shoulderblades and hissed his instructions to me. That's the last I saw of them.

Maybe if I'd practised more with the clutch, the petrol would have lasted longer. Often I had to stay in the lowest gear while the old truck reared and slithered on shoulders of sand, and I gripped the steering-wheel in terror. But even when the track smoothed I couldn't change to a higher gear. Every time I tried, the motor roared and conked out with a lurch. I had to inch along in that low gear, watching the needle on the petrol gauge drop.

When I abandoned the truck I hadn't reached the bridge my father told me to head for. We made the top of a rise before the motor died for the last time. Back towards the west I could see all the ground I'd covered so slowly. And there, near the horizon, I saw the drift of dust that signalled another vehicle chasing me. There was a glint as the sunlight flashed on its windscreen.

Only minutes after that, the first of the banks of huge black clouds rolled over, releasing the stinging cold rain. I knew I wouldn't have the telltale dust as a warning of my pursuers.

But I found the bridge before they found me, and then this old cabin with its faded books. I chose one and started reading. It's a habit I caught from my father. If there's anything in print around he has to read it. Even all the words on the Weetbix packet if the newspaper's late.

I'm glad the books are here. Their words distract me from my fear and from the pain in my feet. My old farm boots suddenly seem to be too small. When I ease them off and push down my socks, I see that each heel has a red weeping patch where blisters have formed and broken.

I haven't any idea how far I am from the border. Get to the bridge, Dad kept saying, as if that would save me, but I know from the map that I'm hardly halfway across the desert. On foot, how long will it take? Three days, a week? Three weeks? I wouldn't survive.

I return to the book I was reading, the one in which I found my name, Solana. Solana's the heroine of the story. She's being chased across a desert.

Solana rocked backwards and forwards in despair, her arms wrapped around herself. She knew she had to continue her journey. It was vital she crossed the border, carried her news to the outside world. But she doubted whether her feet could bear the pain —

I shut the book as if to silence it. I have an eerie sense that it's reading my mind. But it's only a book. It has a blue cloth binding faded to greyness. *Flying East on a Broken Wing* by Bill Tulloch. Published in 1954 in London. The blurb says: "In the early 1990s, when Perth is invaded and Western Australia's government is taken over by an enemy power, the rest of Australia is unable to help — paralysed by fear for the safety of the Western Australians and by the total lack of information or communication from the conflict area. When 14-year-old Solana's activist parents are arrested, she sets off on a daring overland journey east from Perth, driven ever onwards by the need to bring news to the outside world. This is a gripping adventure story about an Australia of the future."

My name, my age, my situation exactly. The enormity of the coincidence is frightening. But that's all it can be: a coincidence. I don't believe in magic.

I flick through the pages to find where I stopped reading. *Solana lifted her head, all her senses suddenly alert. Far in the distance there was the sound of a car engine. It stopped, and Solana heard a car door slam and in the still desert air she heard voices. They were familiar voices. She ran out of the cabin, down through the scrub towards the ravine. Ahead in the swirling mist on the far side was her parents' white station wagon. Beside it she glimpsed the brilliant red of her mother's skirt as she and her father stepped forward to peer down at the remains of the smashed bridge so far below in the angry water. "They must have escaped!" Solana's thoughts were racing. "They followed the same track I did only to find I've destroyed the bridge!"*

Her thoughts were cut off abruptly by the terrifying sound of a helicopter, the rapid throb of blades that had beaten fear into their hearts since the invasion. She saw her parents hurriedly trying to shelter beneath the car but it was too late. A burst of orange machine-gun fire —

I can't bear to read more. I'm remembering that vehicle I saw following me. It must have been my parents. Dad said hardly anyone else knew about the old camel track.

In a panic I struggle into my boots, limp out of the cabin towards the ravine. The book is thrust into my overalls front as if I need it to guide me. Soon I'm going faster as my feet grow numb, or maybe I'm ignoring the pain. And trying to comfort myself with this thought: that book doesn't get everything right. There are no olive trees around the cabin. And the book doesn't say that Solana was sitting in the cabin reading a book about what was happening to her.

It's further to the ravine than I remember. It takes nearly an hour. It's mid-afternoon before I see the two upright poles where the bridge was bolted. I'm looking into the sunlight — there *is* a vehicle on the other bank. Just in time I stop myself from calling, and crouch among the scrub, praying I wasn't seen. It's a jeep, and the two men looking down at the broken bridge are in enemy uniform.

After an eternity they leave. Then, for a long time, I watch the plume of dust following the jeep as it moves into the distance, back to the west.

I'll have to leave the cabin immediately, keep hurrying eastwards. Somehow they've found out about the camel trail. They might have forced my father to tell them. I shiver, not wanting to think about that.

Back towards the cabin in the growing dusk. I plan to stop there only to collect some water. The quarter moon, now gathering strength in the darkening sky, should give me enough light to continue walking during the night, in the coolness.

It's properly dark when I reach the cabin. I stop, horrified — there's smoke gushing from the chimney, startling white smoke lit by the faint moonlight. The windows are flickering gold and orange. There's a man sitting in front of the fire, smoking a pipe, drinking from a mug. He's not in uniform.

I fling open the door and he swings around. I'm ready to run but he doesn't seem threatening, more comic, really, with his astonished eyes behind quaint glasses that remind me of Dad's spares.

"You startled me. Didn't expect a wood sprite to be popping up in these parts." He speaks like our maths teacher, Mr Lyon from Lancashire. The smell of some kind of stew cooking fills the cabin.

He doesn't seem to notice the wary way I'm watching him. He moves a chair back from the table for me to sit on. I should tell him to put out the fire. Enemies might see it.

A wave of pain from my feet hits me, and I ease my boots off, wincing as the blood rushes to my savaged heels. He gives me tea with four spoons of sugar and I talk about my feet. Right now their hurting is the most important thing in my life.

"I've got the stuff for that," he says. "Tramper's Balm. I wouldn't travel half a mile without it in my pack." Incredibly, there's water when he turns on the tap. He moistens a square of cloth and gently bathes my heels. "That'll draw some of the heat out," he says. "You've walked a fair way to do that much damage."

The coolness soothes me, the hot tea makes me relax. My eyelids want to close. Through my lashes I notice how the firelight gleams on the fabric of the curtain and the mattresses, making the spaceships and stars twinkle like real ones. On the table there's one of the tin bowls I used for collecting rainwater. It seems to shine as if he's polished it back to newness. It's full of fresh green olives. Stupid with tiredness, I worry about whether he saved the water that it held before.

I tell him, to keep myself awake, how far I've travelled, about destroying the bridge.

"You just kicked that whole bridge over?" he says admiringly. Then he laughs. "I'm impressed. It looked pretty solid to me."

Talk of the bridge reminds me I have to get going. Enemy soldiers are coming, I warn him. He's surprised — he doesn't seem to know what's been going on. So I tell him about my parents being arrested, my fears, my need to move on — it's amazing that he knows nothing about the invasion. "But then," he says slowly, "I've been hiking through the outback for a fair while." He's looking at me narrow-eyed, speculatively, as if he doesn't know whether to believe me.

Suddenly we both hear it, that dreadful sound, the beating roar of a helicopter. "You see, you see?" I shriek, leaping up. "Now do you believe me? They'll see the smoke — all this firelight — come on!" I rush outside, heedless of my bare feet. All I can think of is to cower in the cover of darkness. But it's not dark outside. There's overwhelming light. I'm blinded for a moment. It's the light from the helicopter's searchlights, and I'm bathed in it.

The noise is hideous. They haven't shot me yet. Perhaps they enjoy watching me hypnotised by terror and light like a possum on the road. Then it's as if the noise lifts for an instant, and I can hear "Solana! Solana!" very faintly — it's my father, suspended on a rope ladder, stretching out his hand to me.

The helicopter starts to rise as soon as I grab his hand. The rope ladder's being drawn upwards. I glimpse my mother's face, the red of her dress. "But Dad, there's someone else in the cabin we should rescue," I sob into his ear as he holds me tightly against the swinging ladder.

"There's no time — those bastards know we've nicked their buzzer. They won't be far behind. We can't stop again!" He's shouting or whispering; I can't distinguish in the continuous explosions of sound.

We swing past the cabin again as the helicopter banks to fly east. But the cabin is dark. There's no trace of smoke, no firelight.

My mother's arms are around me now. "You saw the cabin because of the firelight," I say to her. "And there was me wanting him to put out the fire." My teeth are still clattering, my jaw feels stiff. My father overhears me. I see him look at my mother, a quick look that shows disbelief. I'm right in seeing that because my father says, gently, in a voice to calm me, "We went that way because I knew about that old hut. It made sense you'd shelter there. But no, Solana, it was dark, no fires, dark as doom when we flew towards it."

"But there *was* a fire." I start to say loudly that

the cabin must have signalled itself like a light-house beacon — but already I'm unsure. I don't understand how he could have extinguished those signs of life in so few minutes.

If he hadn't been there, if I hadn't lingered all that time drinking his tea, if I'd kept walking on in the darkness as I'd planned, the helicopter wouldn't have found me.

"I saw my name in this book," I tell them, but I'm too sleepy to continue, cradled and safe now in the sky, heading east. I know the book exists, I'm sure of that. In fact I can feel its sharp edge right now against my chest.

THE MESSAGE
IN THE DUST

I argued for weeks to be taken on this expedition, so I shouldn't start complaining now.

But this dust storm is swirling around and rushing through the canyon. It's coming from every direction as if it wants to attack me, hitting like a hailstorm and hammering at my space helmet. Ahead of me, between the rock walls, I can just make out the figures of Todo and Nadia, but they're getting further away, walking faster, disappearing into the dust storm.

I hate it here, and I wish I hadn't come.

The temperature register attached to the wrist of my spacesuit is telling me it's over 255 degrees Celsius outside. I know the heat can't possibly penetrate through the protective suit, so why do my arms and legs feel as if they're melting? I hope I don't faint. I can imagine the consequences.

Two, three more steps. I've lost sight of Todo. I'm certain there's the taste of hot dust on my tongue. I close my eyes, hoping that I'll get back to normal, that I'll be able to stop imagining that the outside is getting inside my protective suit.

That's when, inside my closed eyes, there's this picture: a pool of water shaded by flowering creepers hanging from the branches of massive trees. It's more than simply a mind picture. I can feel the cool wetness of the water on my skin. Someone's laughing and I can hear too the sound of a waterfall near me.

My eyes spring open and the vision is gone. Again there's the din of the swirling grit on my helmet.

"You'll have to go back and get Pearl. For heaven's sake, Todo, I told you over and over again not to bring your daughter. She's too young to be tagging along on an archaeological expedition. We can't afford the time to be worrying about a kid."

It's Nadia's voice, coming through the radio transmitter inside my helmet. I know that Nadia, in her typically poisonous way, wanted me to hear her words because she could have tuned directly into Todo's transmitter and spoken to him privately.

Nadia's a scientist, an archaeologist like my father, Todo. But I know very well that she fancies him a whole lot, and she's making it clear she didn't expect to have me along on this trip. She thought she'd have Todo all to herself.

Todo's figure takes shape in the whirlwinds of dust. I can't tell from his face through his helmet if he's annoyed at having to come back for me, perhaps already regretting that he gave in to my wish to come with him. But, anyway, he's here, and I take his outstretched hand. I direct my transmitter so my voice reaches him alone. "Thanks, Dad."

We're forced to walk through this canyon with its dust storms because when we arrived on this planet and found the area we'd been directed to, we discovered that even our smallest vehicles wouldn't get through its narrow passage. We couldn't fly in because the savage up-draughts would have smashed our approaching aircraft.

We were able to send the robots in ahead of us, though, and for two days now they've been digging through sand and rubble at a point near the end of the canyon, and building a shelter around their digging area. So, when the three of us finally reach the site, we're standing in a small area of calmness.

I let go of my father's hand and peer into the deep pit the robots have prepared. Even the fierce hot light in the canyon isn't strong enough to reach the bottom.

Nadia's voice again. "Keep Pearl back from the edge, Todo. A broken leg is the last thing we need."

"She's OK, Nadia." He sounds absent-minded. I know he'll be thinking of nothing but what we might find at the base of the pit. He'll be wondering if this is going to be like all the other times, enormous loads of material shifted to reveal nothing. Disappointment. Start all over again. But this time the evidence is very strong — he's sure he's going to find what he's looking for, and it will be where he expects it to be.

I know he's sure, because he's shown me the hundreds of photographic probes we've made as our spaceship approached this planet. The photographic probes are sensitive to organic matter, to living things on planets other than Earth. Todo has this great enthusiasm for finding proof that there's some kind of life out here in the Galaxy.

I watch Todo, aware of what's filling his mind, knowing that he's sure of success with this excavation. For an instant the vision of the waterfall tumbling into the pool flashes into my mind again.

One of the robots extends a platform that lowers us gently into the pit. The light becomes eerie as we go deeper. There's a greenish tinge reflecting from the shiny fabric of our clothing as the darkness grows. Then the robot at the bottom turns on its spotlights. Instantly we're in light as strong and ordinary as sunlight on Earth.

Our platform hovers above the floor of the pit. "Just as we expected," Todo is saying. He reaches out and touches the nearest side of the digging. His glove leaves a tiny indentation, and a trickle of grit slides to the floor. "Soft dusty sand. Hardly compacted at all."

"You're sure we've dug deep enough?" Nadia asks.

"According to the computer estimates, we're standing on what would have been the floor of the canyon around sixteen hundred years ago. Exactly where we want to be."

Todo has explained all this to me. We needed to dig to reach the level that was the floor of the canyon in the year 500. The winds have been filling the canyon with the dusty erosion of its walls during all the years since then, and for who knows how many countless years before that.

It is to this precise spot that our photographic probes have directed us.

It had rained for two nights and two days. She leaned back in the tiny pool, laughing as the cool water splashed on her. She unbraided her hair and let the stream tumbling from the rocks above cascade over her head and shoulders.

By tomorrow, this pool hidden among the cedars and the vines would have drained away into the soft limestone. But the heavy rainfall had added probably six months' supply of water to the reservoir, and had softened the limestone and helped the labour on the foundations for the new temple. Chac, the rain god, must be pleased with the temple, and the workers, and everyone else in the town.

It was getting dark. Along with the evening calls

of the birds and the monkeys she could hear the clinking sounds of the stonemasons dying away as one by one they packed up for the day and returned home.

She should be helping to prepare the evening food. Or grinding the maize for tomorrow. Or collecting the wood for the fire. There were always things to be done to help her mother, boring jobs that had to be done day after day. She envied her brother. He was the one who was allowed to learn the mysteries of their father's craft.

As she braided her hair she heard the sound of one lone carver continuing to work. It was coming from the little quarry at the head of the ravine, her father's favourite workplace. He must be working late. She remembered that he'd asked her to meet him there, tonight, before the stars were lit. She was late.

Vines still wet from the rain swung around her as she ran to the quarry. Her father sat on the ground in an alcove cut into the limestone rockface, tapping gently on a tablet leaning against the wall. A lighted wick flickered in a bowl of maize oil beside him, throwing a moving glow on to the small stone tablet he was carving. In the shadows near him she could see another carving, the one he was preparing for the priest, a centrepiece for the new temple. It was huge, stretching high above her head.

"You haven't done much work on that today," she commented, looking up at the carving. Her father turned quickly, startled at the sound of her voice. He hadn't heard her approach barefooted across the rock. He relaxed when he saw her, and turned back to his work.

She was still peering at the tall carving. "Another feather on the headpiece, one more skull on the chain necklace. The priest's not going to be very pleased with that for a whole day's work." She sat down, leaning against the base of the carving.

"He'd be even less pleased if he saw you draping yourself all over it."

"You're not going to tell him, though, are you, and you're the only one who knows."

"I can't think why you're not at the house doing daughterly things," he said, continuing his tapping on the small tablet.

"Ha ha," she replied. He often said things like that. Mockingly, she said, "I'm here because you ordered me to be here, oh mighty father." She went on, "I've been swimming in the rain pool. And guess what. I had a vision while I was in the water. A kind of awake dream."

He looked at her, now leaning forward with her arms clasped around her knees, her dark eyes wide. "All right, go on, tell me," he said.

"I could see this figure. I think it was a girl, but it was hard to tell because she was covered all over with soft silver. Imagine that. Covered in silver. Like a god. But she can't have been a god, because she was in awful difficulties, struggling in this dreadful heat and dryness through a whirlwind that was almost knocking her over. She could hardly stand up."

"And what happened?"

She sat back. "I'm not sure. I think someone came to rescue her." Her father had stopped carving, was looking troubled. "It's all right, really. It's the dreaming you do when you're asleep that's really significant. I wasn't asleep during that dream. You've always told me the gods only send messages in dreams when we're asleep."

He turned back to his work. "I'm not so sure about that any more," he murmured.

She walked over and put her arms around her father's neck, squeezing him affectionately. "What's this you're working on?" she asked, looking over his shoulder.

She was reading the delicate tracery of curves in small squares that nearly covered the tablet. He sighed. He couldn't stop her. From years of watching him work she'd learned to decipher the glyphs.

She finished reading. He could see in the glow of the little lamp the fear on her face.

"This's unbelievable," she whispered. "Who's this telling you they're going to turn up in a ball made of fire? Are they gods?"

"They must be. They say they come from up there — beyond that group of stars." He pointed to the sky, but she hardly took the time to glance upwards. She was staring at the carved message again.

"How can all this information about the stars help us? And I'm *not* going to believe that our world is round! As far as you can see, even from the top of the old temple, it's flat."

He knew that she was trying to dissuade him from what he had agreed to do. He patted her hand soothingly. "The priest'll understand how to use this information. That's why I asked you to meet me here. I want you to take this to him, and only to him."

"But these gods, they want to take you with them, in exchange for this? If you go, you mightn't ever come back, and that's too high a price to pay for — "

"Listen to me, my nosy girl. If golden explosions from the sky speak to you in a voice you can understand, you don't demand explanations. I think it's reasonable to believe what they say. This voice told me that all our families will die, all our temples will crumble and return to the jungle, unless we understand more about the patterns of the stars. And there's the information the voice gave me, there on that stone tablet. Well, it might be true. It's probably worth a try." He spoke lightly to hide his fear. He knew without a doubt he would never come back.

"So you see," he said, "I have to go with them. I've already promised. It's in return for this wisdom they've given me. You must understand — " he touched his daughter's face gently " — it'll save us all. I think it's tonight they're coming for me."

"But why you?" she said desperately. "Why did they have to choose you? I don't want you to go . . ."

"Well," he said, returning to his casual tone of voice, "I'm the only one around here who can write things down. And anyway, there has to be some drama — fireworks in the sky, a disappearance — or the priests won't believe the words on the stone, will they? They'll think I've made it up. And why would priests believe the words of a humble stonemason?"

He was looking up at the stars and when he spoke again his voice was urgent. "You must take this writing to the priest. Tonight he'll be consecrating the cornerstones for the new temple. You'll find him there." He stood up and hugged her, kissing the top of her head. "Goodbye, my dearest daughter." He loosened the leather thong that held a jade ornament to his earlobe and handed the earring to her. "Keep this to remember me. And I'll take this with me." He tapped sharply at the edge of the carved stone tablet and a small corner fell off into his hand. The fragment of stone he held was covered with the carving of the glyph representing the flower that was her name.

She couldn't speak. She wrapped her fingers around the jade earring. Her father looked upwards again. "Go now! Take the stone and go! Don't look back!" His fear was that if she lingered, the gods from the sky would take her with them as well.

She took the carved stone tablet and ran with it clutched against her chest, ran without daring to look back as she heard the thunderous noise and saw the jungle around her lit by a thousand flashes of lightning. She ran through the town, past the groups of people who stood staring, shocked, waiting to see what disasters the gods were preparing for them. It was as if time had stopped and she was the only one able to move, while all around her were transfixed.

She reached the site of the new temple. She could see the priest at the far corner, surrounded by his bearers, frozen like the people in the town. Below her was the deep excavation for the base of the temple, already partly filled with limestone rubble.

Again she heard the overwhelming thunder. The lightning flashed around her. Terrified, she lost her balance, and fell, down, down into the blackness. Hundreds of loosely balanced rocks tumbled after her, and she died there, buried, with the stone tablet still clutched to her chest and the jade earring held tightly in her left hand.

The priest and his bearers, the people in the town, waited for almost an hour, held still by their fear. Nobody saw her fall. Nobody could explain her disappearance or that of her father. Somebody else finished the tall carving for the priest.

We find it almost immediately. The robots do most of the work. The crumbling grit is gently brushed away and the thing takes shape. Nadia is operating one of the video cameras.

We've found a human male, not very big, curled up like a child asleep on a cold night. He looks as if he is made of very old leather.

"Preserved," Todo says, "in the hot sand."

"Human, would you say?" Nadia says.

"Mmmm." It seems Todo's so pleased he can't speak.

"It is questionable, of course," Nadia continues. "The shape of the head, for instance . . . the rather flattened forehead . . . years of research, I'd say, to get this lot sorted out. And if it is human, well, it's hardly proof of extraterrestrial life, is it?"

"Except, of course, when you wonder how he came to be on this planet." Todo glares at Nadia.

Todo and Nadia talk on about protecting the body for transportation, taking samples of the rock and sand in the area. I can't take my eyes from the small brown man. And then, inside my head, or perhaps it's all around me — I can't tell — the light dims and there's a tiny glow from a candle flame. There's the black glistening head of a girl leaning forward, reading. I can hear and understand the words the girl reads. I see the man beside the girl pass to her the ornament he was wearing on his ear, then the girl is running, desperately, carrying the engraved words. I see her fall.

I'm bewildered and stand there shaking my head. Suddenly the lights are normal again. Todo and Nadia are programming the robots. I check the oxygen gauge on my wrist and the organ function indicators beside it. Everything is as it should be. Heart, lungs, blood pressure, brain patterns are normal. There's nothing to explain these visions.

Our platform is ready to lift us back to the canyon. "Wait!" I shout.

"What now?" Nadia's voice is impatient.

"Over there." I'm pointing to the other side of the digging.

"It's nothing, just a little subsidence from the wall."

"Nadia's right, I think," Todo says. "Yet more dust and rubble, Pearl."

"Let me look."

"OK." Todo moves the platform in the direction I point. Quite clearly, through my transmitter, I hear Nadia's sigh of irritation. I don't take any notice. There's something more important guiding me.

The robot's arm extends with its brush, but I push it aside. I can hear in my head the sharp clink of a mason's chisel against stone. I sift the different textures of dust and grit and small stones and rubble in my fingers, then I find it. It's a triangular piece of stone, its sharp corners eroded away, but the tiny carving on it still easy to see. I gently brush the dust from the carved grooves, and show it to Todo.

"It's a glyph, a Mayan carving," he says slowly.

"It stands for 'waterlily,'" I say faintly, and no one hears me.

"Sixth or seventh century, perhaps," Nadia says. "Well, I suppose that fits in with our estimations."

"Our preserved human," Todo says excitedly. "Of course, he's a Mayan Indian."

"You're right!" says Nadia. "Maybe we're on to an explanation for those huge Mayan temples abandoned in the Central American jungle — all those carved glyphs in a language no one can understand — "

"I can understand the glyphs," I murmur. Again neither of them hears me.

All our families will die, our temples will crumble and be taken over by the jungle — I can hear her father's voice, can read the carvings on the stone, through her eyes, as clearly as if the words were written in my own language.

I close my fingers over the fragment of stone. Waterlily. Somehow she and I have made contact across sixteen centuries.

Todo puts his arm around my shoulders. *"Very good work,"* he says.

Nadia pats my helmet. "Beginner's luck."

We ride up to the surface on the platform. I don't think it's a good idea to say anything more right now. Later I'll tell Todo that it's back on Earth that we'll find the rest of the stone tablet, and that I understand the carved glyphs on it, and that there we'll find the remains of a girl and an earring that belonged to the man we found. I know I'll be able to recognise the place where Waterlily died.

But it's going to be difficult to explain how I know all this.

ABOUT THE AUTHOR

Caroline Macdonald was born in a small town in Taranaki, New Zealand, the youngest by eleven years in a family of four children. By the time she was five, her sisters and brother had grown up and moved away from home, and so she grew up almost as an only child.

Caroline's first book, *Elephant Rock*, was published in 1983, and won for her the Esther Glen Memorial Medal awarded by the New Zealand Library Association. Her second, *Visitors*, was voted New Zealand Children's Story Book of the Year in 1985. Perhaps her greatest success to date has been her post-ecological-disaster novel, *The Lake at the End of the World*, which has received wide commendation: it was winner of the Alan Marshall Award for Children's Literature in the Victorian Premier's

Literary Awards, 1989; an Honour Book in the Children's Book Council of Australia Book of the Year Award (Older Readers), 1989; shortlisted for the New South Wales Premier's Literary Award, 1989; placed in the 1990 Aim Children's Book of the Year in New Zealand; and runner up in the *Guardian* Children's Fiction Award, 1990. Her novel *Speaking to Miranda* was shortlisted for the CBC's Book of the Year Award (Older Readers) for 1991 and also for the 1991 Aim award in New Zealand; and *The Eye Witness* was shortlisted for the Adelaide Festival National Award for fiction for children. Her latest novel is *Secret Lives*.

After years of moving between Australia and New Zealand, Caroline has now settled in South Australia, and lives in the Adelaide Hills.